Enid Blyton

A BOOK
OF
FAIRIES

Enid Blyton

A BOOK
OF
FAIRIES

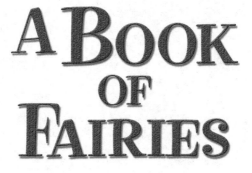

DEAN

EGMONT
We bring stories to life

First published in Great Britain in 1924 by Newnes
This edition published in 2007 by Dean,
an imprint of Egmont UK Limited
239 Kensington High Street, London W8 6SA

Copyright © 2007 Enid Blyton Limited

Enid Blyton's signature is a registered trademark of Enid Blyton Limited,
a Chorion company.

ISBN 978 0 6035 6284 6

1 3 5 7 9 10 8 6 4 2

Printed in Singapore

CONTENTS

Fireworks in Fairyland

ONCE UPON A TIME there lived in Fairyland a number of little workmen, all dressed in bright green. They had very long legs and very sleepy eyes, and they sat in the grass all day to do their work.

They were the fairies' knife-grinders, and whenever a fairy wanted her knife sharpened you could hear the buuzz-z-z of the blunt knife held against the little grindstone that each workman had by him.

The fairies used to bring their knives each morning early, and then, as they were being sharpened, they sat on toadstools and talked.

"The North Wind is in a terrible temper today," said one. "I met him just now."

"Ah!" said one of the knife-grinders. "*I* know why. It's because the late roses came out yesterday in the Queen's garden, and she won't let the North Wind blow till they're over!"

"And he says he *must* blow, else he'll burst himself with keeping all his breath in," went on another workman, stopping his grinding because he was so interested.

"Yesterday I saw Hoo, the White Owl, and he told me a lovely story about those three naughty little gnomes, Ding, Dong, and Dell," began another fairy.

"Oh, do tell us!" begged all the workmen, stopping work at once to listen.

The fairy told them the story, and the workmen forgot all about their knives. When the story came to an end the sun was high in the sky, and it was nearly twelve o'clock.

"Oh, I'm so sleepy!" yawned a knife-grinder, lying down on his back.

"I *can't* finish these knives!" said another, and fell asleep beside his grindstone.

There those lazy little workmen slept soundly until four o'clock, when the Fairy Queen happened to come along, bringing a crowd of elves with her.

"Oh, your Majesty, look here!" cried one, pointing to a sleeping workman. "He's fast asleep, and it's only four o'clock!"

"How disgraceful!" exclaimed the Queen. "And look at all those blunt knives! They ought to have been sharpened long ago! Does this often happen?"

"We don't know," answered the elves, "but Hoo, the White Owl, lives near here, and could tell you."

So Hoo was called and flew silently down to the Queen.

"Yes, your Majesty," he said, in answer to her question, "they are good little workmen, but terribly lazy. They are for ever talking with the fairies, and going to sleep any hour of the day."

"Wake them up," commanded the Queen to her elves. "I can't stop to scold them, but you may stay behind and do it for me."

The Queen flew on and left some of her elves behind.

"We'll give them a fright," whispered the elves. Then each elf flew down beside a workman and shouted a most tremendous shout in his ear. Then, quick as lightning, they hid themselves behind toadstools.

You should have seen those workmen jump! They all woke up at once, nearly jumped out of their skins, and looked all round in great terror.

"What was it?" they all cried.

Out came the elves from behind the toadstools, looking very stern.

"The Queen has just passed," they said, "and found you all asleep with your work not done. She is very cross indeed!"

But the workmen hardly listened. "Was it *you* who woke us up like that?" they asked, looking very fierce.

"Yes, it was, and it serves you right!" answered the elves.

"Then you are very unkind, and we'll pull your ears!" shouted the workmen, rushing at the elves. But, quick as thought, they spread their wings, and flew away, laughing at the angry little knife-grinders.

"It's a *shame*!" stormed one. "Those horrid little elves are *always* playing tricks on us and making us jump!"

"Can't we pay them back somehow and give *them* a fright?" asked another.

"Yes, let's! How could we make them jump just like they made us?"

"I've got a glorious idea!" said another. "Let's go

to the world of boys and girls and get some fireworks. It's November 5th tomorrow and there will be plenty about."

"Yes, and go to the palace and play tricks on those elves with them!" cried all the other workmen, looking really excited.

So it was all arranged. Two workmen were sent off to get rockets, Catherine Wheels, Golden Rain, and jumping squibs from our world. They soon came back with a big sack full of them, and the knife-grinders made all their plans.

Next morning a message came to them from the Queen, saying they must all go to the palace that day, as she was holding a great party and dance for her elves, and wanted all the knives sharpened.

"That's better still!" cried the workmen, and hurried off at once.

They sharpened all the knives very quickly and then asked if they could help lay the table for the feast, and polish the floor for the dancing.

"Certainly!" answered the Head Steward. "You are very good to help us."

So those knife-grinders slipped into the banqueting hall, and began preparing their tricks. They put some crackers in the dishes of sweets and chocolates and some in the middle of a big ice-cream pudding.

"I'm going to put Golden Rain fireworks among all these flowers round the hall!" called a busy workman. "The elves always smell the flowers!"

"And I'm pinning Catherine Wheels on to the wall!" chuckled another. "The elves won't know what they are, and they'll be sure to poke about and see!"

"Look, do look! I've had a glorious idea! I've tied rockets to the front legs of every chair! Won't those elves jump?" called another knife-grinder, looking most delighted.

"Isn't it *lovely*? Won't they be cross? They *will* be sorry they made us jump!" called all the workmen.

"Now we'd better hide somewhere and watch. We'll go behind those big curtains. Have you all got squibs in your pockets?" asked the biggest workman.

"Yes," answered the rest.

"Now, all be quiet whilst I say some magic. We shall have to use some to make the fireworks go off directly anyone touches them."

Everyone was quiet, and the leader sang some queer words.

"There!" he said. "Now, directly anyone *touches* those hidden fireworks, they'll all go off bang! Let's go and hide."

The knife-grinders ran behind the long curtains,

and there they waited till the guests came in to the party.

Soon the elves arrived, all in beautiful dresses and shiny wings. Then came the Queen, and gave the signal for the feast to begin.

Everything went well until an elf asked for some ice-cream pudding. For directly the Head Steward began to put a spoon into it, there came a most tremendous noise!

Crack! Splutter-crack!! Bang!!!

It was the cracker inside the pudding, gone off directly it was touched!

"Oh, oh! What is it?" gasped the Head Steward, looking very astonished.

Then suddenly—

Crack! Bang! Crack!

The elves were helping themselves to chocolates and sweets, and the crackers in the dishes were exploding!

How those elves jumped! And how the naughty little workmen laughed, behind the curtain.

"Someone has been playing tricks," said the Queen, looking rather stern. "If you have all finished, get down, and we will start dancing."

The elves got down, and went into the dancing hall. The workmen followed, making sure no one saw them, and hid behind the curtains there.

"What glorious flowers!" cried the elves, and bent to smell the wonderful roses round the walls.

Fizzle-fizzle-fizz! Whizz-z-z!

Out shot Golden Rain, directly the fairies smelt the roses!

"Oh, what is it?" they cried, falling over one another in their haste to get away. "It must be some new sort of caterpillar! Ugh, how horrid!"

"Yes, and what are those funny curly things on the walls?" asked the Queen.

An elf went up to a Catherine Wheel and poked it with his finger.

Whirr-r-r-r! Whirr-r-r-r!

The wheel spun round and round and shot off sparks!

"Oh, it's alive! it's alive! What is it, what is it?" shouted the elves, crowding together in frightened astonishment.

"Never mind," said the Queen, looking sterner than ever. "Begin your dancing."

The elves began dancing round the room.

"Throw your jumping squibs on the floor!" whispered the biggest workman. "That will make the elves jump!"

Quickly the squibs were thrown on the floor of the hall.

Crack! Splutter-jump! Crack! Jump!!

Those squibs were jumping all over the place!

"Oh! Get off my toe, you horrid thing!"

"Goodness me! Go away, go away!"

"Oh, oh, what are they? They jump us and won't let us dance!"

The elves were really frightened.

"Go and sit down," commanded the Queen, "and I will find out who has done these naughty things."

The elves went to the chairs round the hall and sat down.

Whizz-z-z! Whoosh-sh-sh! Bang!!!

All the rockets tied to the chairs shot up in the air directly they were touched by the elves!

"Oh, oh!" cried the elves, nearly jumping out of their skins with fright.

"Keep where you are," called the Queen, "and see what else happens."

Nothing happened, and the elves began to feel more comfortable.

"Lord High Chamberlain," commanded the Queen, in a dreadfully stern voice, "go and look behind those curtains over there."

The Lord High Chamberlain stepped across and pulled the curtains aside.

And there were all the naughty little green workmen, looking very frightened indeed!

"Come here," said the Queen.

They all came and stood in front of her throne.

"What do you mean by playing such naughty tricks on my elves?" she demanded.

"Please, your Majesty, they made *us* jump the other day, so we thought we'd make *them* jump," answered the biggest workman.

"You know quite well that that's not the right thing to do at all," said the Queen. "I am quite ashamed of you. You are not fit to be in Fairyland. You have spoilt our party and frightened all my elves."

"Oh, please, we *are* sorry now," sobbed the workmen, feeling very miserable.

"You don't do your work well and you are lazy," said the Queen. "I think it would do you good to do some jumping and stretch those long legs of yours a bit. I am going to punish you, and perhaps you will remember another time that I will have no one in my kingdom who does not do his work well and beautifully."

"*Please* let us sharpen the fairies' knives for them," begged the knife-grinders. "We really *will* do it beautifully now."

"Very well, you may still do that," said the Queen, "and as you are so fond of making people jump, you had better jump a lot too."

She waved her wand.

And every little workman there turned into a green grasshopper!

"Go into the fields," said the Queen, "and do your work properly."

All the green grasshoppers turned to go, stretched their long legs, and *jumped* out of the hall! Hop and a jump, and a jump, and out they went into the fields.

They still sharpen the fairies' knives for them, and you can hear their grindstones buzzing in the summer somewhere down in the grass. And when you see them hopping you will know why it is they jump instead of run!

Fireworks are forbidden in Fairyland, now, and I really don't wonder at it, do you?

Betty's Adventure

THERE WAS ONCE upon a time a little girl who didn't believe in fairies. "But, Betty, there *are* fairies, because I've seen them," said her brother Bobby.

"Pooh! You're telling stories!" answered Betty crossly. "There aren't fairies, or gnomes, or elves, or anything like that, so you couldn't have seen any!"

Now the brownies heard her say this, and they determined to teach her a lesson.

"What can we do to show her she's wrong?" asked one.

"Don't you think it would be rather funny if we took her to the middle of Fairyland, where there's crowds of fairies and elves, and see what she says when she sees them?" laughed a merry little brownie.

"Yes, yes! Let's!" cried the others. So they made their plans and waited.

One day Betty was out for a walk by herself, when she saw a big notice up, which said: "PLEASE DO NOT WALK THIS WAY."

"How stupid!" said Betty. "It doesn't look like a

proper notice. I believe it's only a joke. Anyway, I *shall* go that way!"

"We thought she would! We thought she would!" chuckled the brownies, who had put up the notice and were hiding in the bushes.

Betty walked past the notice, and down a little lane. She came to a stream, and by the side of the bank rocked a little golden boat.

"There's no one here! I'll just get in and see how it feels to rock up and down like that!" said Betty. She jumped into the boat and sat down.

Out sprang the brownies, gave the boat a push, and ran back laughing.

Betty didn't see the brownies, and suddenly felt the boat jerk. Then it floated out into midstream, and began going down the river!

"Oh! Oh! Stop! Stop!" cried Betty, feeling frightened. But the boat wouldn't stop. It went by magic. Betty had no oars, and could do nothing.

Presently it passed cottages on each side. Old women in pointed black hats stood at the doors.

"They look just like witches in Bobby's story-book," thought Betty, "but I know they can't be."

On and on the boat went, until Betty, tired with the sun, fell fast asleep. At last the boat stopped with a bump, and Betty woke up. She found the

boat had stopped by some steps, so she got out and ran up them.

"Wherever am I?" she thought. Then she stared in astonishment. She saw a fairy dressed in blue, with long blue wings, coming towards her.

"It can't be a fairy!" thought Betty. "It must be somebody dressed up for fun."

"Welcome to Fairyland!" said the fairy.

"Don't be silly!" said Betty. "There isn't such a place. And what are you dressed up like that for? Is there a fancy-dress party?"

The fairy looked puzzled. "No," she said, "I'm *not* dressed up. I'm just a fairy!"

"You're telling stories!" said Betty rudely. "I shan't speak to you any more!" She walked on by herself, turned a corner, and came straight into a noisy market-place, full of fairies, elves, brownies, and gnomes.

"It *is* a fancy-dress party!" said Betty. "Oh dear! I wish I'd got a fancy dress too, and had been invited!"

"Buy a magic spell?" asked a little brown gnome, running up to her with a tray full of curious packages.

"Oh, don't be silly!" said Betty, getting really cross. "I know you're not real, so you needn't pretend to be! There aren't any fairies!"

All at once there fell a great silence. No one spoke, but everyone turned and looked at Betty in astonishment. Then a grandly dressed fairy, with great wings, stepped over to her.

"You must be making a mistake," she said. "You're in Fairyland, you know, and we think it is very bad manners, besides being very stupid, to say there aren't any fairies when you are surrounded by them."

Betty began to feel alarmed. After all, it didn't really look like a fancy-dress party! Perhaps Bobby *was* right, and there *were* fairies!

But Betty was an obstinate little girl, and she hated to say she was wrong.

"I don't care *what* you say!" she said. "I don't believe in fairies!"

The crowd round her looked angry.

"Call for Giant Putemright!" shouted someone, "and put her in prison till she's a bit more polite!"

Betty felt frightened. She looked round for a way to escape, but there was none. Suddenly there was a shout!

"Here comes Giant Putemright!"

Betty looked and saw a great giant lumbering down the street. She saw everyone was looking at him, and not at her, and she turned and ran away as fast as she could. She ran and ran and ran, till she had no breath left. Then she turned and looked back. Far away she could see a crowd of little people, but they were going a different way.

"They won't catch me after all!" said Betty, sinking down on the grass for a rest. "Oh dear! I don't like this adventure. I *wish* I'd never said I didn't believe in fairies. Why, here's hundreds and hundreds of them; all sorts!"

Just then she heard a little puffing noise. She looked up, and saw near by her a pair of railway lines, and over them was coming a tiny little train. It stopped near her, and the driver leaned out.

"Are you waiting for the train?" he called. "We're going to the Glittering Palace."

Betty jumped up. Yes! She would get in the train, then if the fairies tried to find her any more, she would be far away!

She scrambled into a little carriage and sat down on one of the cushions on the floor. There was a dwarf on another one, but he took no notice of her. The train whistled and went on again.

"What lovely country!" thought Betty as they went through fields of wonderful flowers and past gardens filled with roses.

"Oh! That's the Glittering Palace!" said Betty, as they came in sight of a great shining palace, with turrets and pinnacles gleaming in the sun.

The train stopped and Betty jumped out. "I'd better ask the way home," she thought. She went up to the driver.

"Could you tell me the way out of Fairyland?" she asked.

"No, I couldn't," said the driver. "But if you go and ask at the Glittering Palace, I dare say someone would tell you." He blew the engine's whistle, waved to her, and drove away.

Betty made her way to the Glittering Palace. She came at last to some great open gates. There was no one to speak to, so she went through them and up a great flight of steps. At the top she came to a big hall, hung with wonderful blue curtains.

"My goodness!" whispered Betty, stopping. "Why, I do believe that's the Fairy Queen on that throne, that Bobby talks about such a lot."

Sure enough it was! Around her was a crowd of fairies, and elves, all chattering excitedly.

"Silence!" said the Queen. "Sylfai, you tell me what all this excitement is about."

"If you please, your Majesty," said Sylfai, "there's a horrid little girl come to Fairyland, who doesn't believe in us! She's run away from us, and we thought we ought to come and tell you, so we all flew straight here!"

"Oh! Oh! There she is! There she is!" shouted an elf, pointing at poor Betty. She turned to run, but this time she was not quick enough, and the gnomes surrounded her, and dragged her to the Queen.

"Please! Please! I *do* believe in fairies!" wept Betty. "I'm sorry I said I didn't."

The Queen looked grave. "You're a silly little girl," she said. "Because you can't leave Fairyland now! No one is allowed to if she comes here and disbelieves!"

"Isn't there any way of going back?" asked Betty. "I didn't *mean* to come."

"Yes, there's just one way," said the Queen. "And

that is this: If you know anyone who really *does* believe in fairies, and loves them, he can take you back!"

"Oh, Bobby does, Bobby does!" cried Betty. "Please bring him here!"

The Queen looked at her. "Are you quite sure he does?" she asked. "Because we don't want *two* people here who don't believe."

"Yes, he *does,* he's always talking about you, and how he loves you!" said Betty.

The Queen turned to a gnome.

"Go and fetch Bobby!" she commanded. He sped off.

"Let's have a dance while we're waiting," said a fairy. And they all began dancing in the hall, while the Queen looked on. Suddenly Betty gave a cry of delight.

"Bobby! Bobby!" she called.

And there was dear old Bobby, coming up the hall with the little gnome. He looked delighted to be with the fairies, but most astonished to find Betty there.

Betty told him all her adventures and begged him to take her home again.

"Of course I will, if the Queen will let me," he answered.

"Yes, take Betty home!" said the Queen. "She has

learnt her lesson, but I am sorry she has not had a happy time in Fairyland. Still, it was her own fault. Will you bring her again, Bobby, the next time we have a party, and we'll try to make her love us, as well as believe in us."

"I'd *love* to!" said Bobby, smiling in delight. "What fun! Now then, Betty, hold on to me! I know the way home. Shut your eyes, turn round twice— One, two, three!" and down came a great wind, picked them up and set them down in their very own garden.

Betty rubbed her eyes. "Oh, Bobby!" she said. "I'm so glad you fetched me. I'll always love the fairies now, and oh! won't it be fun to go to their next party?"

"Let's go and tell Mummy," said Bobby excitedly. "My word, *what* an adventure!"

Bufo's One-Legged Stool

ONCE UPON A TIME the King of Fairyland called all his fairy subjects to his palace. They came flying and running in great excitement, wondering why his Majesty should want them.

The King sat on his beautiful, shining throne, waiting until every fairy was there. Then he held up his hand for silence and spoke to them.

"Fairy-folk," he began, "once every year a prize is given to the fairy who thinks of the cleverest idea to make the world more beautiful. Last year, you remember, Morfael won the prize with his golden polish for the buttercups."

"Yes, we remember!" shouted the fairies.

"Well, this year, I'm going to make a change," said the King. "I am going to give the prize to the one who thinks, not of the *cleverest* idea, but of the *most useful!* And please tell the rabbits and frogs and birds about it, because it's quite likely they would think of a good idea just as much as you fairy-folk."

Well, the fairies were most excited. They rushed off telling everyone about it.

"I'm going to think hard for a whole week!" said one.

"And I'm going to use some old magic that will tell me the most useful thing in the world!" said another.

"Let's go and tell all the animals," shouted a third.

So they visited the grey rabbits and told them. They called out the news to the grasshoppers. They gave the message to Hoo, the White Owl of Fairyland, and he promised to tell all the other birds.

"Now I do believe we've told everyone!" said the fairies.

"No, we haven't. What about ugly old Bufo the Toad, who lives on the edge of Fairyland?" asked an elf.

"Pooh! What's the good of telling *him*?" cried a pixie scornfully. "He's so stupid and ugly, he'd *never* think of any good idea. Leave him alone!"

But it happened that next door to Bufo lived a brownie called Bron. He had decided to make a beautiful scarf for fairies to wear when the wind was cold. He thought it would be most useful. He was making it of spiders' webs and thistledown, and as he sat in his little garden at work, he sang a little song:

> *"Oh! I am very wise,*
> *I'm sure to win the prize,*
> *And when I've won the prize, you'll see*
> *How very, very pleased I'll be!"*

Bufo the Toad kept hearing him sing this and at

last he got so curious that he crawled out of his cottage and asked Bron what prize he was singing about.

Bron told him. "The King's giving a prize to anyone bringing him the most *useful* idea this year!" he explained. "Why don't you try, Bufo?"

"I'm so clumsy!" said Bufo. "But I'd like to try all the same. Yes, I think I will."

"I'm making a wonderful scarf for when it's cold!" said Bron proudly. "It's made of cobwebs and thistledown!"

"My! You are clever!" said Bufo. "Now I'm going indoors and try to think of something myself!"

He waddled indoors. His cottage was very queer inside. Bufo was so fat and heavy that he had broken all the chairs and his sofa, through sitting on them too hard! So there were none in his cottage at all. He had a big table, and as he really did want something to sit on, he had made himself one large stool. He was so stupid at making things, that he thought he had better give his stool just one large fat leg in the middle. He was afraid that if he tried to make three legs to it like Bron's smart little stool, he would never get them the same length. So inside his cottage there was only one table and a queer one-legged stool.

Bufo the Toad climbed up on to his stool, shut his great yellow eyes, and thought!

At last he opened his eyes. "I've got an idea!" he cried. "I'll make an eiderdown of pink rose petals! That will be a most useful thing, and it will smell lovely!"

So he hopped out into his garden and collected all the largest rose petals he could find. Then he begged some spider-thread from a spider friend and began.

But poor Bufo was clumsy. He kept breaking the spider's thread, and the wind blew half his rose petals away.

"Ha, ha!" laughed the rude little brownie. "Ha, ha! Bufo! It really is a funny sight to see a great toad sewing rose petals! Don't you worry your stupid old head! *I'm* going to win the prize, I tell you!"

But Bufo wouldn't give up. He went and sat on his stool again and thought. He thought for three days before he found another idea.

That was really rather a good one. He caught a little pink cloud, and decided to stuff a pillow with it. He thought it would be so lovely and soft for fairies' heads.

Bron laughed to see Bufo poking the pink cloud into a big white pillowcase with his great fingers. He called his friends and they came and watched Bufo and teased him.

"Poke it a bit harder, Bufo!" they called over the fence. "It's a naughty little cloud, isn't it? It won't let you win the prize."

Bufo took no notice for a whole day. Then he suddenly got angry, left the half-stuffed pillow on the grass, and hopped to the fence to smack the rude little brownies.

But alas! As soon as the half-stuffed pillow had no one to hold it, the little pink cloud began to rise in the air, to go back to the sky, and it took Bufo's lovely pillow-case with it!

"Oh, oh, now look what you've made me do!" wept Bufo, trying to jump into the air and catch the pillow. But he couldn't, and the naughty little brownies laughed harder than ever.

Bufo went and sat on his stool again. This time he thought for six weeks. When another idea came, he was so stiff with sitting that he could hardly jump off his stool.

"I'll make some wonderful blue paint, to paint the Queen's carriage with!" he decided. "I know it wants repainting, so that will be useful."

He lumbered off with a huge sack. He got the dawn fairies to give him a scraping off the blue of the sky. He asked the blue butterflies for a little powder off their wings. He took one bluebell flower and one harebell. Then he lumbered home again with his sack full of all these things.

When he got indoors, he took a blue shadow, mixed it with honey and water, and poured it into a large paint-pot. Then he emptied his sack into it, and stirred everything up well.

"It's the most glorious blue paint ever I saw!" said Bufo, very pleased. "*This* will be useful, I know."

Now the next day was the day the King had arranged to hold a meeting to judge all the ideas, and everyone in Fairyland was most excited. When the day came, Bufo put his paint outside his cottage door, all ready to take, and then began tidying himself up. Suddenly he heard a terrible yell from Bron, his next door neighbour.

"Help! Help! Arran the Spider is stealing my lovely scarf!"

Bufo rushed out to help, and saw Arran running off

with Bron's scarf. He quickly stopped the spider, and took the scarf away.

"He stole some of my thread," grumbled Arran, running off, frightened. "I thought I'd come and punish him!"

"Oh, thank you for helping me," cried Bron. "If he'd taken my scarf, I wouldn't be able to win the prize."

"Yes, but it's wrong to take Arran's thread, if he didn't want you to," said Bufo severely. "You ought to say you're sorry to him, and give it back!"

He waddled back to his cottage, but, oh! he quite forgot he had put his pot of blue paint outside the door. He walked straight into it, and splish-splash! clitter-clatter! It was all upset.

"Oh! Oh! My beautiful paint!" wept Bufo. "I've spilt it all, and there's no more time to think of other ideas!"

Some fairies passing by stopped to listen.

"You must take *something*, Bufo," they called mischievously. "The King will be cross with you if you don't."

Bufo believed them. "Oh dear! Will he really? But what *shall* I do? I've nothing else but my stool and a table!"

"Take the stool, Bufo!" laughed the fairies, flying on.

So poor old Bufo the Toad went indoors and fetched his one-legged stool, and joined the crowd of flying fairies. How they laughed to see him waddling along carrying a big one-legged stool.

At last they all reached the palace, and the King soon came to hear and to see the useful ideas that the fairy-folk had brought.

"Here's a wonderful necklace made of raindrops!" cried a fairy, kneeling before the King.

"It is beautiful, but not useful!" answered the King gently. "Try again."

"Here's a new sort of polish for the sunset sky!" said the next fairy.

The King looked at it. "That's no better than the one we use now," he said. "Next, please."

Fairy after fairy came, and rabbits and birds and other animals.

Some had beautiful ideas that weren't useful, some had stupid ideas, and some had good ones.

At last Bron's turn came. He showed his beautiful scarf.

"It is lovely, Bron," said the King, "but it is not warm enough to be useful. Also I know you have been unkind to Bufo, and you took Arran's thread without asking. I am not pleased with you. Go away, and do better!"

Bron hung his head and crept away, blushing and ashamed.

At last everyone had shown their ideas, except Bufo. He crawled up to the King and put his one-legged stool down.

"I thought of many ideas, but they all got spoilt," he said. "Is this one any use? It is a good strong stool, easy to make, and quite nice-looking."

The King looked at it thoughtfully. Then the Queen leaned forward and spoke.

"Don't you think, Oberon," she said, "that it is just the thing we want to put in the woods for fairy seats? Think how easy, too, they would be to put up in a ring for a dance!"

31

"Well now, so they would!" said the King. "It really is just what we want. It is certainly the most useful idea we've had given to us today. We could *grow* these one-legged stools by magic in the woods, and use them for tables *or* for stools!"

"Then we'll give Bufo the prize!" said the Queen. "Three cheers for Bufo!"

How surprised the fairies were to see ugly old Bufo win the prize! And oh! how delighted Bufo was! He could hardly believe his ears. He almost cried with joy. He was given a little golden crown to wear, and though he certainly looked rather queer in it, he didn't mind a bit, because he was so very proud of having won it!

One-legged stools were put all about the woods that very day, and they have been used ever since by fairy-folk. Sometimes you find them growing in a ring, and then you'll know there has been a dance the night before.

They are still called toadstools, although it is many, many years ago since Bufo the Toad won the prize. Not many people know why they have such a funny name, but you will be able to tell them the reason now, won't you?

The Wizard's Magic Necklace

"OH DEAR, OH DEAR!" sighed Gillie. "I do wish I wasn't so ugly. My nose is so long and my brown suit is so old!"

Gillie looked at himself in a clear pool of water. He was a little gnome living in Fairyland, and he certainly *was* very ugly.

"Hullo, Gillie!" suddenly called a little voice.

Gillie looked round. He saw his friend the grey rabbit, sitting down among the primroses.

"Hullo, Greyears!" he said. "What have you come to see me for?"

"I've got a letter for you," said Greyears. "It's to say that the rabbits are giving a party tonight, and they want you to come to it. The pixies are coming too, so be sure and look your best, won't you?"

Gillie took the letter and read it.

"How lovely!" he cried. "Thank you so much for asking me. But, oh dear, I *wish* I wasn't so ugly, Greyears!"

"Yes, you are rather ugly," said Greyears, looking at his friend. "But if you bought a new coat, Gillie, and wore some beads or something, you would look *much* nicer."

"I can't have a new suit yet," sighed Gillie. "I've got to wait till next month. And I haven't any beads at all, have you?"

"No," answered Greyears. "But, I say, Gillie! I've got an idea!"

"What is it? Do tell me," begged Gillie.

"Well, come over here, and I'll whisper," said the grey rabbit, looking round to make sure that no one was about.

"Listen. You know where that old wizard Coran lives, don't you? Well, he has got a wonderful necklace. It is all made of yellow and red-brown stones. It would look simply *lovely* on your brown suit, Gillie."

"Oh," said Gillie, "but he wouldn't lend it to me, I know. He's a dreadfully cross wizard."

"Well, if you like, I'll get it for you. I can burrow into the room where he keeps it, and then bring it to you. He will never know. You can easily put it back when you've worn it," said Greyears.

"All right," answered Gillie. "It's very nice of you, Greyears, and I shall look lovely at the party."

"I'll bring it to you tonight, by this little pool," called Greyears, hopping off as fast as he could.

Gillie felt very excited. He took off his little brown suit and mended up the holes beautifully with some spider's thread. He washed off a dirty

34

mark and put it in the sun to dry. Then he sat down by the little pool and waited for Greyears to come back with the necklace.

"How lovely I shall look with a string of yellow and brown stones," he thought. "Oh, here comes Greyears."

Greyears lolloped up to Gillie. He held a glittering necklace in his teeth.

"Oh, Greyears, how beautiful!" cried Gillie, taking it into his hands. "See how the stones shine and glitter. Oh, how beautiful I shall be!"

"Sh!" said Greyears. "Don't talk so loudly, I believe the old wizard heard me. Put on the necklace and come to the party with me, before he finds out it is gone."

Off they both went, and Gillie had a most glorious evening dancing with the pixies. Everyone thought he looked lovely in his beautiful necklace, and he was very happy.

"It *has* been lovely," said Gillie to the grey rabbit as they went home.

"Hark, what's that?" suddenly whispered Greyears.

They both crouched down in some bracken and listened. They heard a curious noise—a sort of panting and groaning.

"It's the wizard," whispered Greyears.

"Oh dear! Has he missed his necklace?" asked Gillie. "Whatever shall I do? He'll be dreadfully angry if he finds me here wearing it."

"Keep still," said Greyears, "and perhaps he won't find us."

They both kept quite still, and presently along came the wizard with his servants. He stopped just by Greyears and Gillie.

"Now then," he cried to his servants in a queer, panting voice. "Now then, hurry up and do what I tell you. That necklace *must* be found. You must search in all the homes of the little gnomes for it."

"Yes, your Excellency," replied the servants.

"I feel sure one of them has got it. Oh dear! Oh dear! I'm much too old to come out at this time of night, all in the dark!" said the wizard, groaning, as he hobbled off away from the bracken where Gillie and Greyears were hiding.

They waited till he was safely out of sight, then they crept from the bracken and looked around. The necklace glittered in the starlight, and Gillie wondered what to do with it.

"Oh dear!" he sighed. "How I wish I hadn't borrowed it. Now I must hide it somewhere till the old wizard has forgotten about it, and then put it back somehow."

"Where will you hide it?" asked Greyears. "Don't

you think it would be better to go and give it to the wizard and say you're sorry?"

"Oh no! I *couldn't!*" said Gillie. "I should be so afraid he would be cross with me."

"Shall I hide it in my burrow for you, Gillie?" asked the grey rabbit.

"No thank you—I know of a much better place. Come with me, Greyears, and I'll show you." And off went the two friends as fast as they could.

At last they came to an old mossy wall. Gillie climbed up, right to the top, and sat there to get his breath.

"There's a big hole here, Greyears," he called, "and I'm going to hide the necklace in it."

"Can I do anything to help you?" asked Greyears.

"Yes, scrape up some earth with your hind legs, and I'll fill the hole with it so that no one can see the necklace shining, if they fly over the wall."

Greyears busily scraped some earth loose. Presently Gillie climbed down, and taking off his brown cap he filled it with earth. Then he climbed up again to the top of the wall.

"That's just enough," he said; "it covers the necklace nicely."

"Plant some flowers along the top!" said Greyears, "then no one will guess what's underneath."

"How clever you are!" exclaimed Gillie, scrambling down again. He looked about for some flowers, and found some tiny white ones with four petals, growing in a hedge. He pulled them up by the roots and climbing up the wall again, he planted them all carefully along the top. Then he slid down to the ground.

"There! *That's* done!" he said. "Thank you for helping me, dear Greyears. Now, let's go home, I'm so tired."

"You can fetch the necklace in a month's time," said Greyears, "and put it back again somehow."

Gillie went to Greyear's burrow for the night, and soon they were both sound asleep.

Gillie didn't go near the old wall at all for a long time. If he had, he would have seen something wonderful happening.

The little white flowers he planted were growing, and were spreading all along the wall—but they were no longer white! They were growing to be great strong flowers, yellow and red-brown like the necklace. They were beautiful in the sun, with their deep colours and soft, velvety petals. They smelt so sweet that some fairies flying by stopped to look at them.

"What lovely flowers!" cried one. "I've never seen any like them before."

"And how *did* they come to be growing there!" said the other. "What a funny place to grow. Let's ask the Queen if she has heard of them?"

But when the Queen came *she* didn't know either, and was very puzzled, because of course she knew the names of all the flowers there were in Fairyland.

"They must be magic flowers," she said at last. "Bring the old wizard here, and ask him if *he* knows what they are."

The old wizard was brought, groaning and panting, and leaning on a strong stick. Just behind came Gillie and Greyears, curious to know what everyone was looking at. They were most astonished to find sturdy yellow and brown flowers growing on the wall.

"Good afternoon, Sir Wizard," said the Queen. "Can you kindly tell me what those flowers are, up there on the wall?"

The wizard looked.

"Good gracious me," he cried, "they're exactly the colour of my lost necklace! That means that they are planted over it, for the stones are magic, and would turn the flowers to yellow and red-brown like themselves."

"Dear me," said the Queen, "but whoever could have put the necklace there?"

"Oh, please, your Majesty, *I* did," said Gillie, kneeling down in front of the Queen, and beginning to cry. He told her all about the party and how he borrowed the necklace.

"But whatever did you want a necklace for?" asked the Queen.

"Because I am so ugly, and I thought it would make me look lovely," sobbed Gillie.

"Why, Gillie, you've a *dear* little face!" said the Queen kindly. "Tell the wizard you're sorry, and I expect he'll forgive you, now he knows where his necklace is."

"Oh yes, I'll forgive Gillie," grunted the wizard.

"Only you must climb up and get my necklace for me again."

"Yes, I will," cried Gillie, climbing up the wall, and sitting among the flowers.

"What shall we call those lovely flowers?" said the Queen.

"Hm! I should call them *wall*-flowers," growled the wizard, "because of where they're growing."

"Yes, we will," said the Queen. "That's a good idea."

And we still call them wallflowers wherever they grow—on the top of a wall, or in the garden beds—and there are some people who call them "*Gillie* flowers," because they remember the naughty little gnome who, years ago, planted the flowers on the wall to hide the necklace of yellow and brown, and so made the very first wallflowers grow.

Lazy Binkity

ONCE UPON A TIME there was a little Brownie called Binkity. He was very lazy and rather naughty, and was always being scolded by the other Brownies.

"Have you tidied up the Oak Tree Wood," asked Ding, the chief Brownie, one day.

"No, I haven't, and I'm not going to!" answered Binkity rudely, and ran away before Ding could catch him. He curled up inside a hollow tree, and watched Ding looking for him, until he was tired and went away. Then Binkity came out of the tree and looked around for something to do.

"Stupid old Ding!" he said to himself. "He's always trying to make me work when I don't want to!"

Then he found a squirrel's hoard of nuts hidden under some leaves at the foot of a tree.

"Ha! Ha!" chuckled Binkity. "I'll hide them somewhere else."

He dug them up quickly, and put them in a rabbit hole. Then he went to find Bushy the Squirrel, who was asleep in a tree.

"Wake up! Wake up!" he cried. "It's a lovely day for a scamper!"

Bushy rubbed his eyes and sat up. "I feel hungry," he said, and down the tree he scampered.

"I'll eat a nut or two," said Bushy, scraping up the leaves at the foot of the tree where he had hidden his nuts.

But they weren't there!

"Oh dear, dear, dear!" cried the squirrel. "Someone's taken them! Whatever shall I do! I *must* have something to eat in the winter!"

Binkity sat on a twig and laughed to see Bushy looking for nuts that weren't there.

Just then Ding, the chief Brownie, came by, with a crowd of other Brownies, and asked Bushy why he was looking so miserable.

"Someone's taken my nuts," explained poor Bushy, "and that horrid little Binkity keeps laughing at me."

"Here are your nuts!" called a Brownie, who had accidentally found them in the rabbit hole where Binkity had put them. "Binkity must have put them there, he's *always* playing tricks!"

Binkity began to feel he had better run away again, and looked round to see where he could go to.

"Binkity!" said Ding very sternly. "You must be punished. You are lazy and mischievous and never help anyone in anything. I shall send you as a servant to Arran the Spider, and he will make you work really hard and keep you out of mischief!"

Now this was a terrible threat, for Arran the Spider sometimes ate people who didn't work hard enough, and Binkity was dreadfully frightened.

He jumped up, and ran away as fast as ever he could, with all the Brownies after him. It was getting dark, and he hoped that soon they would find it too dark to chase him.

"Catch him! Catch him!" called the Brownies, racing after naughty Binkity.

Binkity rushed right through the wood and out into some fields. Then it began to snow hard, and the snowflakes beat against the Brownie's face till he was cold and tired out. But still he could hear the other Brownies chasing him.

"Ah, there's a cottage!" suddenly panted Binkity, as he saw a light near by. He ran up to the cottage, and quick as lightning changed himself into a puppydog.

All the other Brownies, seeing only a shivering puppy, raced by without stopping.

"Now I'm safe," thought Binkity, "but, oh dear, how cold and wet I am!" He began to make a little whining noise, like a puppy.

Presently the door opened and a little girl peeped out.

"Oh, here's a poor little puppy!" she cried, picking Binkity up and taking him in.

She set him down before a fire, and gave him a saucer of milk to lap. When he was quite dry and warm, she took him over to her mother, who was in bed, looking very ill.

"Dear little puppy!" said the mother, stroking him. "I wonder where he came from, Jean. We must keep him, if no one comes to claim him."

Binkity lay down by the fire, warm and drowsy, and listened to Jean and her mother talking. Presently he was astonished to hear the mother crying.

"Oh, Jean darling," she was saying, "I am so ill I cannot get up again this winter, and that means you will have all the housework to do, and all the washing. You will have to do most of the sewing too, to make money, for I am too tired even for that!" And the poor woman sobbed as if her heart would break.

"Never mind, Mother," said the little girl bravely, "I will do my best. Don't cry, we shall be all right." But Binkity could see that she looked dreadfully worried, and he was very sorry for her.

"I wonder if I could help her," he thought, "she has been so kind to me. I daren't change back into a Brownie in the daytime, in case the other Brownies see me. I must still be a puppy, till they have forgotten I was naughty. But at night! Yes! At night, I will change back into a Brownie, and do all the work!"

Binkity was so excited with his idea, that he could hardly wait until the house was dark and still.

When Jean had gone to bed and everything was still, Binkity changed into his own shape again. Then he bustled about the house, making no noise at all. He dusted and washed and tidied till the house was as clean as a new pin. Then, just as dawn came in at the windows, he changed into a puppy again and lay down by the fire.

When Jean woke up and looked round, she could hardly believe her eyes.

"Mother! Mother!" she cried. "Look, look! The house is clean. There is no work to do! I can spend all the day sewing!"

"Jean, it's a Brownie!" said her mother in delight. "There must have been one near here, working in the night. Leave a saucer of milk on the hearth every night when you go to bed, and don't peep to see what happens when you're in bed."

All that day Jean sewed at beautiful tablecloths and curtains, which she sold in the town for money, and when night came she put a saucer of milk on the hearth.

"There! That's for you, whoever you are, little Brownie," she called.

She patted the puppy and kissed him, never dreaming *he* was the little Brownie, and then she went to bed.

All that night Binkity, changed into a Brownie again, did the housework, and even baked some bread for Jean! Then at dawn he changed into a puppy again, and lay by the fire.

"The Brownie's been here again, Mother," said Jean, next morning, delightedly, "and he's done all the work! *Isn't* it lovely!"

All through the winter Binkity lived at the little cottage. Jean and her mother loved the little puppy that jumped around them in the daytime, and never guessed he was really a Brownie. And every night, when Binkity became himself again, he did all the housework and worked harder than he had ever worked before in his life. He loved Jean, and was always delighted to see how surprised she was each morning.

In the spring Jean's mother got better, and was able to get up. Binkity began to feel that he would like to live in the woods again, and talk to the birds and animals as he used to do, and to live in his little Tree House.

"I think I *must* go back now!" he said to himself one night as he was washing the floor. "Perhaps the Brownies will have forgotten they were going to give me to Arran the Spider. Jean's mother can do the housework now, and I'll see that Jean always has plenty of money."

So when the dawn came Binkity, instead of changing into a puppy again, slipped out of the cottage and ran back to his home in the woods.

"Oh, it's lovely to hear the birds again, and to talk to the rabbits!" said Binkity, thoroughly enjoying himself.

"Hullo, Binkity!" suddenly exclaimed a voice. Binkity turned round, and to his dismay found it was Ding, the chief Brownie.

"Oh, please don't send me to Arran the Spider!" he begged, kneeling down.

Ding smiled kindly. "Why, Binkity," he said, "I'm ever so pleased with you! I know where you were all the winter, and I've often peeped into the cottage at night, and seen you scrubbing the floors."

"Oh, have you?" cried Binkity, most astonished.

"Yes, often," answered Ding. "You used to be lazy and naughty, but you've learnt to work hard, and to help other people now. We're going to have a party tonight to welcome you back to Oak Tree Town again."

"Oh, how lovely!" cried Binkity, delighted. He ran off to get himself clean and tidy, thinking it was really much more fun to be a good Brownie than a lazy one.

Jean was very astonished and sorry to find the little puppy was gone that morning, but her mother said it *must* have been a Brownie living with them. Binkity kept his word, and often used to go and visit the cottage and see that Jean was quite all right, and sometimes leave a shining gold piece under her pillow, for a surprise.

He's never lazy now, and if ever you come across a very neat and tidy wood, look about for Binkity. He's sure to be hiding somewhere about, watching you with his little twinkling eyes!

The Lost Golden Ball

THERE WAS GREAT excitement in Fairyland. The Queen's heralds had just gone through the streets of the chief town, and blown on their silver trumpets, to say that every fairy was to go to the big market-place, and wait there for the Queen to come.

"Oyez, oyez, oyez!" they cried. "Her Majesty wishes to speak with you all at half-past nine this morning!"

"What *can* it be about!" cried the excited fairies, gathering here and there in little crowds. "Perhaps someone's been naughty. Or perhaps the Queen wants us to do something for her!"

"Ding, dong, ding, dong!" chimed all the bluebells suddenly.

"Quarter-past nine!" called the fairies to each other. "Come along to the market-place, everybody. The Queen will be coming in a few minutes!"

Off flew fairies and elves, and off ran pixies, gnomes, and brownies as fast as ever they could. Presently a great crowd was gathered in the marketplace, all wondering what their Queen wanted them for.

"Ding, dong, ding, dong! Ding, dong, ding, dong!" chimed the bluebells round about.

"Half-past nine! Here she comes! Isn't she beautiful? Hip, hip, hurrah!" cheered the fairies as the Queen flew down to the throne set high in the middle of the market-place.

"Good-day to you all!" she said, in her clear silvery voice, when all the fairies were quiet and not a sound could be heard. "I have come to ask your help. You all know that the Prince of Dreamland has been staying here, and has lately gone back to his own country."

"Yes, yes, your Majesty!" answered the listening fairies.

"He carried with him a bright golden ball which had, closely hidden inside it, the secret of a new magic spell. It is a wonderful spell which he hoped would make his ill Princess well again. You all know she has been ill?"

"Yes, your Majesty, and we are very sorry," called the fairies.

"On his way home," went on the Queen, "his carriage was drawn by six white rabbits. Suddenly a dog began barking in the distance, and the rabbits were so frightened that they ran away, and in their fear upset the carriage. In the confusion and muddle the golden ball was lost, and the Prince of Dreamland cannot find it anywhere. Will you help to find it?"

"Oh yes, we'd love to, your Majesty!" answered all the fairies in great excitement.

"Very well. Go now, and seek for it," commanded the Queen. "You must find it today, for the spell inside the ball will be no use tomorrow. It must be used before the moon is full."

Off went all the fairies, helter-skelter, through the woods and lanes.

"I shall look in all the long grass!" said Fairy Rosemary. "I am sure I shall find it!"

"*I* shall look in all the little pools!" said a yellow pixie. "It might easily have rolled into one, and be hidden there! Come along and help me, pixie-folk!"

"*We* are going to hunt in the squirrels' nests!" shouted the frolicking elves. "We think the squirrels might have found it and hidden it!"

"Where are *you* going to look, Karin?" shouted the brownies, speaking to an ugly little gnome who was sitting on a mossy stone, thinking.

"I think I shall look under the gorse bushes," said Karin.

"Pooh! Fancy looking there! You'll get pricked all over. You *are* a silly-billy," sang the brownies, dancing round Karin and laughing.

Karin hated being laughed at. He was a shy little gnome, ugly and clumsy. He couldn't do the dainty things his comrades did. He looked so funny when he tried to dance, that, although the fairies tried not to, they simply *couldn't* help laughing. And when he began to sing, everybody flew away as fast as they could. This hurt him very much.

"Why don't they love me and want to be with me?" he used to think sadly, going off by himself.

He was too shy to ask the other fairies and gnomes to be his friends and to like him. He was *much* too shy to tell them he loved them, and as nobody ever guessed what he thought, Karin was always left alone, for everyone thought he was cross and surly, and didn't want to make friends.

"Oh dear!" said Karin sadly to himself, as the brownies ran off to look for the golden ball. "Why does everybody laugh at me and nobody want me to come with them. I *wish* I wasn't ugly and stupid!"

He wandered off by himself, looking for a gorse bush to peep underneath. He found one, and lay down in the grass to wriggle underneath it. It was very prickly and very horrid.

"Ha, ha, ha! Ho, ho, ho!" suddenly laughed someone. "Karin the Gnome, what in the world are you doing? Do you want to find out if prickles are prickly?"

"Bother!" thought Karin, wriggling out again. "Someone or other is *always* laughing at me."

He sat up on the grass and brushed away the bits of gorse that had clung to him. Then he looked to see who had spoken.

It was Hoo, the White Owl. He was sitting on a hazel tree, and looking very much amused.

"It isn't nice of you to laugh at me," said Karin. "I hate being laughed at. I was only looking for the golden ball that the Prince of Dreamland lost."

"A golden ball!" said Hoo. "Well, now I believe *I* know where that is."

"Oh, do tell me!" begged Karin excitedly. "You can't *think* how I'd love to take it to the dear Queen."

"Well, I'm sorry I laughed at you just now, if you

didn't like it," said Hoo. "And to show you I'm sorry I'll tell you where I saw the golden ball."

"Oh, thank you, thank you!" said Karin gratefully. "Whisper in my ear, Hoo."

So Hoo flew down and whispered in Karin's ear. "As I flew by the heath the other night, I saw something gleaming in the moonlight. It was rolling along by itself, and I knew it was magic. I watched where it went, and I saw it roll down beneath a silver birch tree, under a piece of bracken by the bank where Greyears the rabbit lives. You will find it there!"

"Thank you, *ever* so much," said Karin, jumping up excitedly.

"Tu-whit, tu-whit, don't mention it," called Hoo, flying off silently into the trees.

"Hurrah! Hurrah! I'll find the ball! What fun!" thought Karin, running as hard as he could over the grass. The bank where Greyears lived was a long long way away, and he knew he would have to hurry.

He came to the heath. It was a big common called Hampstead Heath, stretching away in the distance. To Karin's surprise it was packed with crowds and crowds of people, some walking, some sitting, and some picnicking.

He hid behind a tree and watched. Although he didn't know it, it was Whit-Monday and everyone had come out into the sunshine, away from the shops, away from the busy towns, and from the stuffy offices. There were children everywhere, running, laughing and playing. Mothers sat here and there and fathers played cricket with the boys.

"Dear me, what a crowd of people!" thought Karin, "and how happy they all look!"

He watched them for some time, then decided he must go on his way. He slipped from bush to bush and tree to tree, unseen, wrapping his green cloak closely round his red jacket and brown knickers. He passed many groups of happy children on his way across the heath, but none of them saw him.

As he glided behind a gorse bush, he stopped suddenly and slipped to the other side. There was a little girl behind it, sitting on the grass and crying. He didn't want her to see him. He was going on his way, when an extra large sob from the little girl stopped him.

"I wonder what's the matter with her!" said Karin to himself, peeping round the bush.

She was a dear little girl. She had short curly hair, big blue eyes filled with tears, and a crying, drooping mouth.

"I want my Mummy," she kept saying. "I want my Mummy! I'm so lonely, I *do* want my Mummy!"

Here was somebody else who was lonely besides Karin, and Karin, who knew how miserable it was to feel lonely was dreadfully sorry for the little girl. He wondered if his ugly face would frighten her if he spoke to her. He decided to try.

He slipped out from behind the gorse bush and stood in front of her. She looked up, surprised.

"Oh," she said, "what a *dear* little man! I'm sure you're a fairy, aren't you?"

Karin was so astonished to hear anyone call him a *dear* little man that he couldn't say anything, but just stood and smiled delightedly.

The little girl put up her hand and stroked him. "I'm *so* glad to see you," she said. "I was just wishing a fairy or something would come and help me."

"What's the matter with you?" asked Karin, finding his voice at last. "I heard you crying!"

"Well, I'm lost!" said the little girl, her eyes filling with tears again. "I'm Ann, and I've lost my Mummy in all that crowd, and I can't find her."

"I'm so sorry," said Karin.

"But you'll find her for me, won't you?" said the little girl, cheering up. "Fairies can do anything, you know!"

Karin stared at her. "I'm afraid I can't stop any longer!" he said. "You see, I'm doing something very important today. Else I *would* have stopped."

The little girl began to cry again. "Aren't I important too?" she sobbed. "You aren't the nice kind fairy I thought you were. I'm *s'prised* at you. I really am!"

Karin couldn't bear to see her cry. He sat down by her and put his arms round her.

"Don't cry, little girl," he said, "I'll give my important business to somebody else to do, then I can stay and help you."

"Oh, you *darling,*" said Ann, and kissed him. "I love you ever-so."

Karin was filled with delight to hear her say so. He never remembered hearing anyone say that to him before. He thought children must be simply lovely, if they went about loving everybody like that.

"I will be dreadfully disappointed not to find the golden ball and to let someone else get it," he thought. "But if this little girl wants me, I don't mind giving up finding it—at least, I don't mind *very* much!"

He told Ann to stay where she was, and running to a pixie he saw by some bracken, he shouted to him:

"Hoo told me where the golden ball was. It's under the bracken by the birch tree growing near the bank where Greyears lives!"

At once the pixie darted off delightedly, and Karin returned to the little girl.

"I've told someone else my important business," he said. "Now, tell me what your mother's like and I'll go and find her."

"She's got curly brown hair and kind eyes," said Ann, "and she's got a lovely purple hat with big red roses on it, and a purple coat!"

"Oh, I'll be sure to find her easily," said Karin. "Stay here till I come back."

"I'll eat my dinner while you're gone," said Ann, opening a little basket of sandwiches. "Would you like some to take with you?"

"No, thank you," said Karin. "I don't think I should like your food very much. You eat it all yourself!"

"You *are* a kind little man," said Ann, giving him a hug. "I really think you've got the kindest face I ever saw."

Karin was so delighted to hear anyone praise his ugly face and call it kind, that he almost shouted for joy. He ran off happily.

He searched and searched for a long time, but nowhere did he see a lady with a purple hat and red roses. There were plenty of red roses but no purple hats.

"Oh dear! Oh dear! I *must* find Ann's mother," said Karin desperately. At last he went back to Ann, to see what she was doing.

She was fast asleep.

"I'll go and have another look," said Karin, who was getting very tired of searching all over the crowded heath. "I do hope I find her mother this time."

As he wandered over the heath again, looking round him as he went, he suddenly saw a very sad-looking lady who was also looking all round *her* as she went. He looked at her hat. It was purple with red roses, and her coat was purple too! It must be Ann's mother.

Karin hurried up to her. "Please," he said, "are you looking for Ann?"

"Yes, yes, I am!" answered the lady, not seeming at all surprised to see Karin. "Oh, do you know where she is? Pray, pray take me to my little girl quickly! Is she all right?"

"Quite all right," said Karin. "Follow me." He walked off quickly in the direction of Ann's gorse bush, and the mother followed closely behind. On the way a pixie popped his head from behind a piece of bracken and called to Karin:

"I went to the bank where Greyears lives, but I couldn't find the golden ball, Karin."

"Oh, I'm sorry. I expect someone else found it!" answered Karin, hurrying on.

At last they reached the place where Ann was. She was just waking up. As she heard their footsteps, she looked up and saw her mother.

"Mummy! Mummy!" she cried, flinging herself into her mother's arms. "Oh, Mummy, I'm so glad it's you. I lost you and I've been so lonely!"

The mother clasped her little girl close, as though she would never let her go, and kissed her curly head again and again.

"That dear, kind little man helped me!" said Ann. "Oh, you dear fairy, I want to give you something. I found it this morning, and it's *ever* so pretty. I'd love to keep it for myself, but I want to give it to you because you've been so nice and I love you. Look!" and she took something from her little basket and held it out to Karin.

It was the Prince of Dreamland's lost golden ball!

"I found it under some bracken by a birch tree!" said the little girl. "I want *you* to have it, Karin."

Karin was so astonished and delighted that he could hardly say thank you. He gave Ann a hug, took the ball, said goodbye, and ran off as fast as he could, thinking that surely children were the very nicest things in all the world.

He ran and ran and ran, hoping he would get to the market-place where all the fairies were to meet, before it was too late. As he came near, he saw hundreds of fairy-folk gathered there and the Queen was speaking.

"Thank you all for looking," she was saying. "I am dreadfully sorry nobody found the golden ball, but I expect one of the crowd of people who came to

Hampstead Heath today found it instead. I do wish I knew where it was."

"Here it is! Here it is!" suddenly called an excited voice. All the fairies turned and saw Karin making his way to the Queen, holding in his right hand a wonderful golden ball.

"Karin! Karin's got it! Fancy, Karin's found it!" cried all the fairies to each other.

"Oh, Karin, how lovely!" said the Queen gladly. "Where *did* you get it?"

Then Karin knelt down and told all the story of

the day's happenings.

"You have done well!" said the Queen. "You gave up something you wanted for the sake of a little girl, and lo and behold, the little girl gave you what you thought you had given up—the golden ball! It was a good reward for unselfishness. Now tell me, what wish shall I grant you for bringing me the golden ball!"

"Oh, please, your Majesty, let me go and play on Hampstead Heath with the children!" begged Karin. "I believe they'd love me, and I *do* so want to be loved. I don't think they'd mind my ugly face. And I'd love to find their mothers for them when they're lost!"

The Queen smiled. "We'll all love you, now we know you want to be loved," she said. "Yes, you may go and live on Hampstead Heath and look after the children there, Karin!"

And Karin can be found there to this very day. No child need fear being lost, for Karin will be sure to help him somehow, whether the child sees him or not! He is as happy as can be, for all the children love him, and he is happiest of all on Bank Holidays, for then he has so many children to look after, he hardly knows where to begin!

Pinkity and Old Mother Ribbony Rose

ONCE UPON A TIME there lived an old witch called Mother Ribbony Rose. She kept a shop just on the borders of Fairyland, and because she sold such lovely things, the fairies allowed her to live there in peace.

She was very, very old, and very, very clever, but she wasn't very good. She was never kind to her neighbour, the Bee-Woman, and never helped the Balloon-Man, who lived across the road, and who was often very poor indeed when no one came to buy his lovely balloons.

But her shop was simply lovely. She sold ribbons, but they weren't just ordinary ribbons. There were blue ribbons, made of the mist that hangs over faraway hills, and sea-green ribbons embroidered with the diamond sparkles that glitter on sunny water. There were big broad ribbons of shiny silk, and tiny delicate ribbons of frosted spider's thread, and wonderful ribbons that tied their own bows.

The fairies and elves loved Mother Ribbony

Rose's shop, and often used to come and buy there, whenever a fairy dance was going to be held and they wanted pretty things to wear.

One day Mother Ribbony Rose was very busy indeed.

"Good morning, Fairy Jasmin," she said, as a tall fairy, dressed in yellow, came into her shop. "What can I get you today?"

"Good morning, Mother Ribbony Rose," answered Jasmin politely. She didn't like the old witch a bit, but that didn't make any difference, she was always polite to her. "I would like to see the newest yellow ribbon you have, please, to match the dress I've got on today."

Mother Ribbony Rose pulled out a drawer full of yellow ribbons. Daffodil-yellows, orange-yellows, primrose-yellows, and all shining like gold.

"Here's a beauty!" said she, taking up a broad ribbon. "Would you like that?"

"No, thank you," answered Jasmin, "I want something narrower."

The witch pulled out another drawer and scattered the ribbons on the counter.

"Ah, here's one I like ever so!" exclaimed Jasmin, lifting up a long thin piece of yellow ribbon, just the colour of her dress. "How much is it?"

"Two pieces of gold," answered Mother Ribbony Rose.

"Oh dear, you're terribly expensive," sighed Jasmin as she paid the money and took the ribbon.

Mother Ribbony Rose looked at all the dozens of ribbons scattered over the counter.

"Pinkity, Pinkity, Pinkity," she called in a sharp voice.

Out of the back of the shop came a tiny gnome.

"Roll up all these ribbons quickly, before anyone else comes in," ordered Mother Ribbony Rose, going into the garden.

Pinkity began rolling them up one by one. He did it beautifully, and so quickly that it was a marvel to watch him.

When all the ribbons were done, he went to the window and looked out. He saw fairies, gnomes, and pixies playing in the fields and meadows.

"Oh dear, dear, dear!" suddenly said Pinkity in a woebegone voice. "How I would love to go and play with the fairies. I'm so *tired* of rolling up ribbons." A large tear rolled down his cheek, and dropped with a splash on the floor.

"What's the matter, Pinkity?" suddenly asked a little voice.

Pinkity jumped and looked round. He saw a tiny fairy who had come into the shop and was waiting to be served.

"I'm so tired of doing nothing but roll up ribbons all day," explained Pinkity.

"Well, why don't you do something else?" asked the fairy.

"That's the worst of it. I've never done anything else all my life but roll up ribbons in Mother Ribbony's shop, and I *can't* do anything else. I can't paint, I can't dance, and I can't sing! All the other fairies would laugh at me if I went to play with them, for I wouldn't even know *how* to play!" sobbed Pinkity.

"Oh yes, you would! Come and try," said the little fairy, feeling very sorry for the lonely little gnome.

"Come and try! Come and try *what?*" suddenly said Mother Ribbony's voice, as she came in at the door.

"I was just asking Pinkity if he would come and play with us," answered the little fairy, feeling rather afraid of the witch's cross looks.

Mother Ribbony Rose snorted.

"Pinkity belongs to *me*," she said, "and he's much too busy in the shop, rolling up my beautiful ribbons all day, to have time to go and play with *you*. Besides, no one is allowed in Fairyland unless they can do some sort of work, and Pinkity can do nothing but roll up ribbons! I'm the only person who would keep him for that, for no one in Fairyland keeps a ribbon shop." And the old witch pulled one of Pinkity's big ears.

"I should run away," whispered the little fairy to Pinkity when her back was turned.

"I wish I could! But I've nowhere to run to!" whispered back Pinkity in despair.

At that moment there came the sound of carriage wheels down the cobbled street, and old Mother

Ribbony Rose poked her head out to see who it was.

"Mercy on us! It's the Lord High Chancellor of Fairyland, and he's coming here! Make haste, Pinkity, and get a chair for him!" cried the old witch, in a great flurry.

Sure enough it was.

The Chancellor strode into the shop, very tall and handsome, and sat down in the chair.

"Good morning," he said. "The King and Queen are holding a dance tonight, and they are going to make the wood gay with ribbons and hang fairy lamps on them. The Queen has asked me to come and choose the ribbons for her. Will you show me some, please?"

"Certainly, certainly, your Highness!" answered Mother Ribbony Rose, pulling out drawer after drawer of gay ribbons. Pinkity sighed as he watched her unroll ribbon after ribbon, and show it to the Chancellor.

"Oh dear! I'm sure it will take me hours and *hours* to roll up all that ribbon!" he thought to himself sadly.

"This is wonderful ribbon!" said the Chancellor admiringly. "I'll have fifty yards of this and fifty yards of that. Oh, and I'll have a hundred yards of this glorious silver ribbon! It's just like moonlight. And send a hundred yards of this pink ribbon, please, too, and I'll have a ribbon archway with mauve lamps made, leading from the Palace to the wood. The Queen will be delighted!"

"Certainly!" answered the witch, feeling excited to think of all the gold she would get for such a lot of ribbon. "The pink ribbon is very expensive, your Highness. It's made of pink sunset clouds, mixed with almond blossom. I've only just got a hundred yards left!"

"That will just do," said the Chancellor, getting up to go. "Send it all to the Palace, please. And don't forget the *pink* ribbon, it's most important, *most* important!"

And off the Chancellor went to his carriage again.

Mother Ribbony Rose, who cared for gold more than she cared for anything else in the world, rubbed her hands together with delight.

"Now then, Pinkity!" she called. "Come here and roll up all this ribbon I've been showing to the Chancellor, and measure out all that he wants!"

Pinkity began rolling up the ribbon. He did it as quickly as ever he could, but even then it took him a long time. He measured out all the many yards that the Chancellor wanted, and folded them neatly. Then he got some paper and began to make out the bill.

"Hullo," said Pinkity, "the inkpot's empty. I must

get the ink bottle down and fill it!"

He climbed up to the shelf where the big bottle of black ink was kept, and took hold of it.

But alas! Poor Pinkity slipped, and down fell the big bottle of ink on to the counter, where all the Chancellor's ribbon was neatly folded in piles! The cork came out, and before Pinkity knew what was happening all the ink upset itself on to the lovely ribbon, and stained it black in great patches.

In came old Mother Ribbony Rose.

"Pinkity! Pinkity! Look what you've done! And I haven't any more of that pink ribbon! You did it on purpose, I know you did, you naughty, naughty little gnome!" stormed the witch, stamping up and down.

Pinkity was dreadfully frightened. He was so frightened that, without thinking what he was doing, he jumped clean through the window and ran away!

He ran and ran and ran.

Then he lay down beneath a hedge and rested. Then he ran and ran and ran again, until it was night.

At last he came to a beautiful garden, lit by the moon, and quite empty, save for lovely flowers. It was the Queen's garden, but Pinkity did not know it.

"I'm free! I'm free!" cried Pinkity, throwing his hat in the air. "There's a dear little hole beneath this rock, and I'll hide there, and I'll NEVER go back to Mother Ribbony Rose."

He crept beneath the rock, shut his eyes and fell fast asleep.

Next morning he heard fairies in the garden, and they were all talking excitedly.

"Yes, it was a naughty little gnome called Pinkity, who spoilt all the Queen's lovely ribbon," said one fairy.

"Yes, and he did it on purpose, old Mother Ribbony Rose says. Just fancy that!" said another.

"And the Chancellor says if anyone catches him, they're to take him to the Palace to be punished, and given back to Mother Ribbony Rose," said a third.

Pinkity lay and listened, and felt the tears rolling down his cheeks. He had so hoped that perhaps the fairies would help him.

All that day Pinkity hid, and at night he crept out into the lovely garden, and the flowers gave him honey to eat, for they were sorry for him.

For a long time Pinkity hid every day and only came out at night. One day he heard a group of fairy gardeners near by, talking hard.

"What *are* we to do about those little ferns?" they said. "Directly they come up, their tiny fronds are spread out, and the frost *always* comes and bites them, and then they look horrid. It's just the same with the bracken over there!"

"It's so difficult to fold the fronds up tightly," said the fern fairies. "They *will* keep coming undone!"

"Well, we *must* think of something," said the gardeners decidedly. "The Queen simply loves her fernery, and she will be so upset if the frost bites the ferns again this year. Let's go and ask the rose gardeners if they can give us any hints."

That night Pinkity went over to the baby ferns and bracken and looked at them carefully. It was a very frosty night, and they looked very cold and pinched.

"*I* know! I know!" cried Pinkity, clapping his hands. "I'll *roll* them up like ribbons, and then they'll be quite warm and safe, and won't come undone till the frost is gone!"

So Pinkity started rolling each fern frond up carefully. It wasn't as easy as rolling ribbon, for the fronds had lots of little bits to tuck in, but he worked hard and managed it beautifully. The baby ferns were very grateful, and so was the bracken.

"Thank you, thank you," they murmured. "We love being rolled up, and we're much warmer now."

Pinkity worked all night, and just as daylight

came, he finished the very last piece of bracken and ran back to his hole to hide.

At six o'clock along came the gardeners. They stared and stared and stared at the ferns.

"Whatever has happened to them!" cried they in

amazement. "They're rolled up just like ribbon!"

"What a splendid idea!" said the Head Gardener. "But who did it? Someone very kind and very clever must have done it!"

"*Who* did it? *Who* did it?" cried everyone.

Pinkity, trembling with excitement, crept out of his hiding-place.

"If you please," he said, "*I* did it!"

"Why, Pinkity! It's Pinkity, the naughty little gnome!" cried the fairies.

"I wasn't really naughty," said Pinkity. "The ink spilt by accident on the ribbon. I wouldn't have spoilt the dear Queen's ribbon for anything in the world."

"Well, you've been so kind to our ferns," said the fairies, "that we believe you. But how *did* you learn to be so clever, Pinkity?"

"I'm not clever *really,*" said Pinkity, "but I can roll up ribbons nicely—it's the only thing I *can* do—so it was easy to roll up the ferns."

The fairies liked the shy little gnome, and took him in to breakfast with them. In the middle of it in walked Her Majesty the Queen!

"*Who* has looked after my baby ferns?" she asked in a pleased voice.

"Pinkity has! Pinkity has!" cried the fairies, pushing Pinkity forward. Then they told the Queen all about him.

"It was quite an accident that your lovely ribbon was spoilt," said Pinkity, "and I was dreadfully sorry, your Majesty."

"I'm quite *sure* it was an accident," said the Queen kindly, "and I have found out that all Mother Ribbony Rose cares about is gold, so I am sending her right away from Fairyland, and you need never go back!"

"Oh, how lovely!" cried Pinkity joyfully.

"Your Majesty! Let him look after the ferns and bracken, and teach other fairies how to roll up the baby ones!" begged the fairies. "He *is* so clever at it."

"Will you do that for us, Pinkity?" said the Queen.

"Oh, your Majesty, I would *love* it!" answered Pinkity joyfully, feeling happier than ever he had been in his life before.

He began his work that very day, and always and always now you will find that fern fronds are rolled up as tight as can be, just like the ribbon Pinkity rolled up at the ribbon shop.

As for old Mother Ribbony Rose, she was driven right away from Fairyland, and sent to live in the Land of Deep Regrets, and nobody has ever heard of her since.

The Floppety Castle and the Goblin Cave

ONCE UPON A TIME there was a little boy who wandered into Fairyland quite by mistake.

"Goodness me!" he said to himself. "Wherever have I got to?"

"Why, you're in Fairyland, of course," said a tiny voice. "What's your name?"

"My name's David," answered the little boy, looking round for the voice.

"Well, here I am, David," laughed the voice; "down here, in a buttercup."

David looked and saw a tiny blue fairy standing up in a buttercup.

"How tiny you are!" he said. "Please, could you tell me the way out of Fairyland?"

"Why, David, what a funny boy you are! It isn't many children who go to Fairyland, and now you are lucky enough to be here, why don't you look round and see some of the wonderful things?" asked the little fairy, swinging himself in the buttercup.

"Oh, I'd love to," said David. "Do tell me

which way to go."

"Well, I should go to that cottage over there, if I were you, and ask for Tom the Piper's Son. He'll go round with you, and show you things," answered the fairy.

"Yes, I will. Goodbye," said David. And off he ran.

When he reached the little cottage, he knocked at the door. A boy, dressed in a blue coat and purple knickers, opened it. "Please, are you Tom the Piper's Son?" asked David.

"Yes," answered Tom, staring at David. "What do you want?"

"I've just come to Fairyland," said David, "and I'm wondering if you'd show me some of the wonderful things here."

"Certainly," answered Tom, looking pleased. "Just wait till I get my pig." He ran in, and in a minute came out, carrying a little fat pig under his arm.

David wanted to ask if the pig was the one that Tom stole, but he didn't quite like to. The pig blinked at him, and grunted.

"Now, what shall we see first?" said Tom. "How would you like to see the Floppety Castle?"

"I'd *love* to," said David, thinking it sounded lovely.

"All right," said Tom, putting the pig down. "Now then, get on his back and hold tight. He'll take us there in a jiffy."

David was rather astonished, but he got on the pig. The little animal didn't seem to mind their weight at all. He trotted off at a great pace. Presently a queer looking castle came in sight.

"There's the Floppety Castle," said Tom.

"Why is it called that?" asked David, holding on more tightly to the pig, who was going faster.

"Ah, ha! You'll see when you get there!" said Tom. "It's a great joke, I can tell you!"

When they reached the castle gate. Tom picked up the pig again and carried him. Into the castle they went.

"I'll wait for you here," said Tom, and stopped by the door.

David wandered in, looking around him as he went. There were curious pictures of kings and queens on the walls, with heads at the top and at the bottom too. Presently he came to a gnome writing at a table.

"Oh, don't shake, don't shake!" cried the gnome, looking up. "What clumsy feet you have! You'll bring the castle down, if you don't look out!"

"Don't be silly," said David, "I couldn't possibly!" And off he went to another room. Here he found a lot of little gnomes busily sorting out a pile of old books. There were so many left about the floor that David tripped over one and fell bang! on the ground.

"Oh, oh!" cried the gnomes, looking terrified. "How clumsy you are! You'll break the castle to bits!"

"Why do you say that?" asked David, picking himself up.

"Well, it's only a card castle, you know," answered the gnomes.

"Goodness me!" said David, looking round. "How very dangerous! Oh, so that's why there are such funny king and queen pictures on the walls. They're cards!"

David quickly turned to go back to Tom, and ran out of the room, feeling that at any moment such a wobbly sort of castle might fall to bits.

But alas! As he ran, he bumped into a passage wall, and crash! clitter-clatter! Down came the Floppety Castle on top of him! When it had stopped falling, David blinked his eyes, and looked round him. There was nothing but a great mass of higgledy-piggledy cards lying about. The gnomes were busy setting some of them up again.

"Oh dear, oh dear!" cried one. "That's the third time this week that the castle has fallen down!"

"Well, why do you build it of such silly things?" asked David, feeling rather cross with fright. "You know it will only fall down again."

"Oh, hush!" said Tom, who came up just then. "You'll hurt their feelings. Do you know why it is called 'Floppety Castle' now, David?"

"Oh yes!" said David, beginning to laugh. "It's really rather funny, you know, to go into a castle and knock it all down!"

"Come on with me," said Tom, still carrying his

pig. "We'll leave the gnomes to build their castle again."

He went off with David, talking merrily. Suddenly he stopped and said:

"David! There's the butcher coming that I stole the pig from! Let's run away, quick!"

Off he went, as fast as he could, and David followed him. The butcher saw them, and chased after them, shouting.

Tom jumped over a hedge, and popped a purple berry into his mouth.

"Quick!" he said. "Eat one, David!"

David ate one—and found himself growing smaller and smaller until he was just as small as the daisies in the grass.

Tom ran down a hole in the bank, and pulled David after him just as the butcher jumped over the hedge.

"Wherever have they vanished to!" they heard him exclaim in wonder.

"I think you ought to have given him the pig back," said David after a while.

"Bless you, *this* isn't his pig! That's eaten long ago! This is my own pig, but whenever that butcher sees me, he remembers the pig I took long ago, and chases after me to whip me!" explained Tom, hugging his pig under his arm.

"Oh, I see," said David, feeling glad the pig really wasn't a stolen one. "Where are we going to?"

"I don't know," answered Tom. "The goblins live down here, but they know me, so I don't think we shall come to any harm."

They soon heard a hammering and a clattering, and came to a great cave, lighted by big star-shaped lamps. In the cave sat hundreds of goblins, making glittering things.

"Why, they're brooches and necklaces!" cried David. "How lovely they are!"

The goblins looked up and smiled. "Thank you for those kind words, little Master," said the chief. "Choose which you will have."

"Oh, thank you!" cried David. "I'd like that tiny brooch shaped like a star, to take home for my mother, please."

"Here you are!" said the chief gnome, fastening it on his coat. "It is a magic brooch, and has two wishes for the wearer."

"How lovely!" said David, as he went out of the cave with Tom and the pig.

Soon the three were quite lost. Cave after cave they wandered through, some brightly lighted, some quite dark. At last, in despair, Tom said, "Oh, use one of your magic brooch wishes, David! Rub it and wish."

"That's a good idea!" said David. He rubbed the little brooch. "I wish we could find our way out," he said loudly.

Immediately there came a little fluttering sound by them, and David saw an elf, dressed in blue and with mauve wings.

"Come with me!" she cried, and led them up a long dark passage into the open air again.

"Goodbye!" she called, and left them.

"Eat some berries, David, to make you big again," said Tom, giving one to his pig.

"Oh, it does feel funny to grow big suddenly!" said David. "It's like going up in a lift! Wherever are we now? I say, the sun is setting and I *must* go home. Do tell me the way, Tom."

"I don't know it," said Tom, putting down his pig. "I'm lost too. Why don't you wish yourself home? You've got another wish. I'm going to get on my pig. He *always* knows the way back to my cottage. Goodbye. See you again another day, perhaps!" And Tom and the pig galloped off, and were soon lost to sight.

"It must be rather nice to have a pig like that," thought David. "Now I'll use my last wish. I *wish* I were home again." And he rubbed the brooch. "Why, goodness gracious! How *did* I get here? I'm at my front gate, and there's Mother looking for me," he exclaimed a moment later, rubbing his eyes.

His mother *was* astonished to hear where he had been, and she simply loved the starry brooch that the goblins made. She always wears it at David's parties, and then he tells the other children of all the lovely things he did with Tom the Piper's Son in Fairyland.

Two Fairy Wishes

JACK AND ANN were digging in the garden. Ann's spade suddenly struck something hard.

"Oh, Jack!" she said, in an excited voice. "My spade knocked something! Do you think it is a box of gold?"

"Perhaps it is," said Jack. "Dig it up quickly and see."

Ann dug it up. It was not a box, but a big bottle with a cork. Jack took the bottle and looked at it. Then he pulled the cork out, and

CRASH!   BANG!   PHIZZ-Z-Z-Z! !

What do you think came out of it? Why, a great long fairy with wings and a crown!

Jack and Ann were too afraid to speak at first. Then the fairy said:

"I have been a prisoner in that bottle for a hundred years. I am very grateful to you both for making me free again; a bad witch put me there, and I could not get out. What would you like me to do for you?"

"Oh," said Jack, "could you give us a wish each? We should so like to wish for something and know it would come true."

"Very well," said the fairy. He waved his wand, and said some queer, magic words. "There!" he said. "I have given you one wish each. Be careful what you wish. Goodbye!" And away he flew.

Ann and Jack were so excited and happy. "What shall we wish?" asked Ann. "Let's ask for something lovely, like wings to fly with."

"Let's think hard," said Jack. They both sat down and began to think of all the lovely things they wanted.

Then Nurse came down the path towards them. "Come along, children," she called. "It's tea-time, and you must wash your hands."

"Oh, Nurse, we *can't* come yet," Jack called back.

"Yes, dear, you must come at once," said Nurse firmly.

"Oh, I *wish* you'd go right away!" said Jack in a temper.

And all at once, in front of their eyes, Nurse was swished right away into the air! Jack had forgotten that he was wishing. The fairy had promised that whatever he wished should come true, and so it had. Poor Nurse was taken right away somewhere.

Jack and Ann were very unhappy and afraid. They ran in to tell Mummy all about it, and to ask her what they should do. Mummy looked very sorry and said she hoped Nurse was not feeling unhappy too.

"Did you say the fairy gave you a wish each?" she asked.

"Yes," said Jack.

91

"Then Ann has still her wish left. You must wish for Nurse to be brought back again," said Mummy.

"Oh, yes," said Ann, "of course I can. I *wish* that Nurse would come back again to us," she said in a loud voice.

And there was Nurse walking into the room! How glad they all were to see her, and Jack said he didn't mind losing the two wishes a bit, now that Nurse had come back again!

The Green Necklace

"OH DEAR ME!" cried Marjorie sadly. "I've lost my dear little green necklace! Wherever can it be?"

She ran up and down the field and looked and looked, but it was all no use, she couldn't find the necklace.

"What are you looking for?" asked a deep voice.

Marjorie looked all round in astonishment. Then she saw a large white owl sitting on a gate looking solemnly at her.

"Did you speak?" she asked in astonishment.

"Yes," answered the owl, blinking. "I'm Hoo, the White Owl, and I belong to Fairyland. Who are you?"

"I'm Marjorie, and I've lost my green necklace," Marjorie explained.

"A necklace did you say? Oh, I know who took that," said Hoo.

"Do you?" cried Marjorie. "Do tell me who it was!"

"Well, it was a fairy called Briony," said Hoo. "He was polishing up the beetles in this field, and suddenly saw your necklace. He was so pleased with it that he took it straight off to Fairyland. He'll give it back if you ask him."

"Oh, thank you for telling me," said Marjorie. "Could you tell me how to find Briony?"

"Certainly," said Hoo, spreading his big wings. "Do you see that mushroom growing down there? Well, break off a piece and rub it between your hands. Say 'Acrall-da-farray' three times, and see what happens. Goodbye and good luck!" And off went Hoo into the trees.

Marjorie quickly broke a piece off the mushroom and rubbed it between her fingers.

"Acrall-da-farray! Acrall-da-farray! Acrall-da-farray!" she said loudly.

Then suddenly a great wind came round about her, and she gasped for breath and shut her eyes.

"Goodness!" she cried when she opened them again. "Why, I'm not even as tall as that mushroom! How small I've gone!"

She found she was standing in the middle of a tiny little path. She followed it for some way, between grasses which waved above her head, until she came to a large toadstool. To her surprise, it had a little door, two windows, and a tiny chimney at the top! Lying in the grass was a small ladder.

Marjorie took the ladder and propped it up against the toadstool. Then she ran up the little sloping ladder and knocked at the door.

"Come in!" cried a voice.

Marjorie opened the door and looked inside. She saw, sitting by the fire, a pixie with large ears and tiny wings. He was playing tunes on a long flutelike pipe.

"Good morning," said Marjorie politely. "Could you tell me where I can find Briony?"

"No, I can't," answered the pixie, "but if you go to the Big Sleepy Sloo, he'll soon tell you. He's a great friend of Briony's."

"Where does the Big Sleepy Sloo live?" asked Marjorie, wondering whatever such a creature was like.

"He lives down in the Glittering Cavern," answered the pixie, getting up. "I'll show you the way."

He lifted a mat up from the floor and uncovered a trap-door. He pulled it up, and Marjorie saw a long slanting passage stretching downwards.

"I'll just play a tune on my pipe," said the pixie.

"What for?" asked Marjorie.

"Well, the only thing that ever wakes the Big Sleepy Sloo is music!" explained the pixie. "He likes *my* music best of all. I'm the Pixie Piper."

He put his long pipe to his mouth and blew. Marjorie thought she had never heard such sweet music. It was like the rippling stream and the rustling trees.

"There!" he said at last. "He'll be awake now. Sit down and slide. You can't walk down such a slippery passage."

Marjorie stepped over the trap-door and sat down at the top of the passage. The Pixie Piper gave her a push and down she went, whizzing along at a tremendous pace. Gradually she slid more and more slowly, and in the distance she could see something bright and dazzling.

"I expect that's the Glittering Cavern," she said. "I hope Big Sleepy Sloo is awake."

She slid straight into a large, shiny cave. All the walls glittered and sparkled, and the floor shone like gold. In the middle sat a queer mouse-like creature, blinking its eyes and yawning.

"Hullo!" he said. "I thought it was the Pixie Piper coming down. What do you want?"

"Please can you tell me where Briony is?" asked Marjorie.

"Yes. He's gone to the Simple Witch to learn how to turn his legs into a tail when he wants to," answered the Sleepy Sloo. "He's thinking of staying with the mermaids for a bit."

"How can I get to the Simple Witch?" asked Marjorie, beginning to feel she would never find Briony.

"Catch the next train that comes along here," said the Sloo, pointing to one end of the cave. To

Marjorie's astonishment she saw a little pair of rails!

Then puff, puff, puff! Choo, choo, choo!
It sounded as if a train were coming already. Sure
enough there was! The queerest little engine
suddenly appeared, dragging two carriages.
It stopped just in the cave.

"Any passengers?" called the engine-driver.

"Yes!" cried Marjorie, hurrying across and
jumping into a carriage.

"Get out at Breezy Hill!" shouted the Sleepy Sloo. "Goodbye!"

"Goodbye!" called Marjorie, sitting down on a fat yellow cushion as there were no seats.

Off went the train into a dark passage. There were only two other passengers. One was a goblin reading a large Fairyland newspaper, and he never spoke a word the whole time. The other was a fat, grey mole, who sat on two cushions.

"Where are you going?" he asked.

"To the Simple Witch," answered Marjorie. "Where are *you* going?"

"To the Fiddlestick Field," said the mole, and fell fast asleep.

The train stopped at a wooden platform on which the name "Goblin Corner" was painted. The goblin folded up his newspaper and jumped out. On went the train and suddenly came out into green fields and sunshine. The next station was Fiddlestick Field, and Marjorie shook the sleeping mole.

"Get out," she cried. He woke up suddenly and climbed out *just* in time, without even saying thank you!

"Well, I don't think much of goblins and moles!" said Marjorie as the train went on.

It climbed up a steep hill, and stopped on the very top. A strong wind blew all round.

"I'm sure this is Breezy Hill!" said Marjorie, and looking out she saw it was.

She jumped out and wondered which way she should go. Then seeing a round hut a little way off, she went up to it, and knocked on the door.

"Come in!" cried a voice.

Marjorie walked in and found an old, old woman stirring something in a pot over a fire. In a corner sat a fairy.

"Good morning," said Marjorie. "Is this where the Simple Witch lives?"

"Yes. *I'm* the Simple Witch," said the old woman, "and that is Briony."

"Oh, I'm *so* glad I've found you at last!" cried Marjorie. "Please, will you give me back my green necklace you found this morning?"

"Rog the Giant has got it," said Briony. "I'm so sorry. I gave it to him this morning. Never mind. Would you like a mermaid's tail instead?"

"Oh no, thank you," said Marjorie. "I'd much rather keep my own legs."

"I'm just learning how to get a tail," said Briony proudly. "It's great fun. But hark! That sounds like Rog!"

They all ran outside. There stood a huge giant, crying great tears and sobbing bitterly.

"It's broken!" he cried. "It's broken!"

"Oh dear! He's broken your necklace," said Briony. "He wore it as a ring, you know. It just fitted his little finger nicely!"

"Never mind," shouted the Simple Witch to Rog. "I'll give you a magic pin instead."

The giant stopped crying and smiled. Marjorie thought he must be very stupid to cry so easily.

"Where did the necklace break?" she asked Rog. "In the field," answered Rog, pointing. Marjorie ran into the field near-by and there, just by the gate, she found her broken necklace. She quickly picked it up and found the beads which had rolled here and there. Then she turned to go back to Briony.

"Good gracious! Where have they all gone?" she cried. "And where is the Simple Witch's hut?"

"Why, it's the field where I lost my necklace this morning!" she exclaimed.

"Tu-whit, tu-whit!" said someone by her, and turning round, she saw Hoo, the White Owl, sitting on the gate.

"Oh, *do* tell me how I got here like this?" Marjorie begged him, quite puzzled.

"Tu-whit, tu-whit!" answered the owl. And not another word would he say.

"Well, anyway, I've got my necklace back!" said Marjorie, laughing, and ran off home.

A Fairy Punishment

THERE WAS ONCE a little girl called Peggy, who didn't always tell the truth. There came a day when she did a foolish and a dangerous thing—she told an untruth to a fairy!

She was playing in the garden, when she saw something lying on the ground.

"Whatever is it?" cried Peggy, as she picked it up. "Oh, it's a dear little fairy hat! I'll keep it for one of my dolls to wear!" She put it into her pocket, and was just going up the path to fetch her doll, when along came a fairy.

"Please, have you seen my hat anywhere in your garden?" she asked. "It must have fallen off somewhere about here."

Now Peggy badly wanted that little hat for her doll. "Oh no!" she said boldly. "I haven't seen your hat anywhere."

Suddenly there arose a faint singing noise from all the flowers round about.

"She has! She has! She has!" they whispered. "It's in her pocket, look and see."

Peggy was very frightened when she heard the

flowers speaking and telling the truth. She took the hat from her pocket, and flung it on the ground.

"There's your old hat," she said angrily.

"Oh, Peggy, did you tell me an untruth?" asked the fairy sadly. "Don't you know what happens when a mortal child tells an untruth to a fairy?"

"No, I don't know and I don't care!" answered Peggy rudely.

The fairy waved her wand. Immediately there appeared four little gnomes, who caught hold of Peggy, and marched her off down the garden path, singing a queer song:

> *"To the Land of Pretence she must go,*
> *And there she will more truthful grow."*

Peggy struggled hard to get free and run away, but it was of no use, she couldn't, and at last the gnomes came to the garden wall.

Peggy suddenly saw a door in the wall that she was *sure* had never been there before. The door slowly opened, and Peggy and the four gnomes entered. Instead of going into the field which Peggy knew lay on the other side of the wall, they went down a long narrow passage, lit by swinging lamps.

"Here's Fairyland," said the gnomes, as they came to the end of the passage and stepped into a cool wood where fairies, pixies, and elves flew about and peepe‹ at them from behind every tree and flower.

The gnomes marched Peggy steadily through the wood, until they came to a wide river on which rocked a yellow boat. Sitting in the boat was a beautiful fairy, dressed in pure white, with silver wings. She had clear blue eyes and the loveliest smile in the world.

"Here is Peggy, Your Highness," said the four gnomes, bowing low.

"Get into the boat," said the fairy to Peggy. Peggy stepped into it. The four gnomes turned, waved goodbye, and ran off through the wood.

"Where are you taking me?" asked Peggy.

"To the Land of Pretence," answered the fairy, as the boat slid off down the river.

"But I don't want to go there, I want to go home!" said poor Peggy, beginning to cry.

"You can go home when you have learnt that truth is the only thing that matters," said the fairy sternly. "You have told untruths to your mother and to your nurse, and to your school-fellows, and your teachers. They have all believed you. Now you are going to a land where you will speak the truth and *nobody will believe you!*"

"Then I shan't speak the truth if nobody will believe me!" wept Peggy.

"I am Fairy Truth," said the fairy. "If you ever want

my help come and look for me by the river."

"I never want to see you again," sobbed Peggy. "I think you're horrid, horrid, horrid! I'll *never* come and look for you."

Just then the boat bumped against a little landing-place.

"Here you are," said Fairy Truth. "Jump out, Peggy."

Peggy jumped out without another word, and ran down the little path that led away from the river.

Coming towards her was a band of gaudily dressed little creatures, half-fairies and half-dwarfs.

"Are you Peggy?" they asked. "If you are, we've come to take you to our Palace to stay with us."

Peggy thought that would be very nice. "Yes, I am Peggy," she answered.

The little creatures looked at her.

Then they pointed their fingers at her and laughed.

"No, you're not! No, you're not! We don't believe you! Your eyes are red, and you've come from the Land of Cry Babies! You're not Peggy, you're a Cry Baby!" they shouted.

Peggy turned and ran right away from them. She ran and ran until she came to a little blue house in the middle of a wood.

She knocked at the door.

"Come in," said a voice. Peggy went in. She saw

three little old women, sitting by the fire, knitting red stockings.

"Who are you?" they asked.

"I'm Peggy, and I've come from the land of boys and girls," said Peggy.

"We don't believe you," said the old women. "We believe you're a naughty runaway fairy. You can stay with us if you do our housework for us."

"Oh dear!" thought Peggy. "Fairy Truth *said* no one would believe me if I spoke the truth, and no one will. How I wish I'd never told an untruth!"

Peggy stayed with the three old women, and was soon busy making their beds and dusting the room for them.

"Have you dusted the tops of the pictures?" asked the old women.

"Yes," answered Peggy, quite truthfully.

"We don't believe you!" cried the old women. "Dust them at once."

Poor Peggy had to dust them all again.

"Are you hungry?" they asked, after Peggy had worked hard for a long time.

"Yes, very," said Peggy.

"You're not telling the truth, we know you're not!" cried the old women. "You say you're hungry just because you're greedy. We shan't give you anything to eat, so there!"

Peggy felt very miserable to think that everything she said was disbelieved. She made up her mind that *next* time the old women asked her anything, she *wouldn't* tell the truth.

"Are you tired?" they asked her, when the night began to fall.

Peggy was dreadfully tired—but she knew they wouldn't believe her if she said so—so she sighed and said, "Oh no!—I'm not tired at all."

"We believe you!" cried the old women. "As you're not tired, you can stay up all night and peel these potatoes."

"I don't want to," said poor Peggy, beginning to cry.

"But you must, you must!" said the old women, and they all went to bed, and left Peggy sitting at the kitchen table, with a huge bowl of unpeeled potatoes in front of her.

"I wish I'd never told an untruth in my life," sobbed Peggy. "I wish I was at home, where everyone believes me, I'd never, never tell stories again. Nobody's kind to me here."

She peeled a few potatoes. Then she threw down the knife.

"I'll go and find Fairy Truth. She had a kind face, and if I tell her I'm ever so sorry, perhaps she'll take me back home again," said Peggy.

She stole out of the cottage and ran through the dark wood. At last she came to a little path, and she ran along this till she came to the shining river. There, sitting in her boat, was Fairy Truth.

"Oh, I'm so glad to see you," cried Peggy, jumping into the boat. "I've come to say I'm sorry I've been rude to you, and sorry I was untruthful. Do take me away from this land, it's awful to tell the truth and not be believed!"

Fairy Truth smiled at Peggy, and kissed her. "I've been waiting here for you. You have learnt your lesson, and now I will take you home."

Up the river went the little boat, and Peggy watched the banks slip by.

"Oh," she cried suddenly, "this is the river that runs in the fields behind our house! And look! Oh look! There's my home!"

"Jump out, Peggy," said the fairy. "Goodbye, and always remember that Truth is the only thing that really matters."

"I'll never, never forget!" cried Peggy, hugging the fairy and jumping out.

Off she ran, over the fields, up the garden, and into her house. And you can just guess how astonished her mother was to hear of all her adventures.

"I'm never, never going to tell a story again," said Peggy, "and I'll never, never go to that nasty old Land of Pretence!"

And you may be quite sure she never did!

The Search for Giant Osta

SYLFAI WAS READING all by herself in the nursery, when there came a knock at the window.

"Goodness me, whoever's that?" thought Sylfai, getting up to see.

The knocking came again. Sylfai opened the window wide and looked out.

"Mind your head!" cried a little voice, and in flew a fairy dressed in yellow.

"I'm Corovell," she said, "and I've come to ask you something."

"What is it?" asked Sylfai, staring at Corovell in astonishment.

"Well, a friend of mine is lying in a magic sleep in Giant Osta's castle. Giant Osta is dreadfully upset, because he's a good giant, and he thinks Peronel, my friend, must have offended someone and had a spell put on her."

"But why have you come to *me*?" asked Sylfai, looking puzzled.

"Well, because the spell can only be broken by someone called Sylfai, and that's *your* name, isn't it?" asked Corovell.

"Yes, it is. Am I going to Fairyland, then?" said Sylfai, feeling tremendously excited.

"I'll take you now," said Corovell. "Shut your eyes and count three, and hold on to me."

"One, two, three!" counted Sylfai, holding on tight. Then she opened her eyes.

"Oh!" she cried. "Oh, why I'm in Fairyland! However did I get here?"

She stood in a beautiful wood, with large toadstools standing about here and there. Corovell stood by her side.

"Now listen, Sylfai," she said. "I'm not allowed to come with you. You must find the way to Osta's by yourself. But I'll give you a piece of advice. If ever you feel cross with anyone in Fairyland say something nice."

"I'll try and remember," said Sylfai, "but I wish you were coming with me."

"Goodbye," called Corovell, and off she flew.

"Dear me, she hasn't even told me which way to go," said Sylfai, looking around. "Well, I shall have to sit down on one of these big toadstools, and wait for someone to come along."

She chose a large toadstool and sat down. Presently, to her astonishment, she saw a large green frog hop up on to another toadstool, and sit down there.

"Please," said Sylfai, "will you tell me the way to Giant Osta's?"

The frog blinked at her, but made no answer.

Then Sylfai saw a large green caterpillar crawl up on to another toadstool and curl itself round.

"Will *you* tell me the way?" she asked.

Still there was no answer.

Then on a third toadstool up hopped a great green grasshopper. He stared solemnly at Sylfai, but wouldn't speak a word.

Suddenly a cross voice made Sylfai jump. "Now then!" it hissed. "Get off my seat!"

Sylfai looked down and saw a long green snake sliding round about her toadstool.

"This isn't your seat!" she said. "I got here first."

Then the frog, the caterpillar, and the grasshopper all spoke at once—"Push her off, push her off, push her off!" they cried in a sort of chorus.

Sylfai was going to say something very cross indeed, when she remembered Corovell's advice, and tried to think of something nice instead.

"Oh, I'm sorry if I am sitting on your toadstool," she said politely. "I'll get down." And off she jumped.

The grass snake wriggled up and curled himself on the top.

"You *are* polite," he said, "instead of being cross

and rude. We belong to a Green Club because we are all green and meet here to talk on the toadstools every evening. Can we help you in any way?"

"Well," said Sylfai, feeling very glad she had been polite, "can you tell me the way to Giant Osta's?"

The caterpillar raised itself up, and spoke:

"I have eaten cabbages in Osta's garden," he said. "I can tell you part of the way."

"Oh, please do!" begged Sylfai.

"Well, go through the wood until you come to a little wooden house painted yellow. In it there lives a dwarf who will take you part of the way. Tell him Greenskin of the Green Club sent you."

"Thank you," said Sylfai, taking a last look at the queer members of the Green Club, and off she went through the wood.

Presently she came to a wooden house, painted yellow. Sylfai walked round it, looking for the door—but to her astonishment there *was* no door! and only one tiny window, very high up.

Sylfai knocked loudly on the walls.

"Come in, come in," cried a voice.

"I *can't* come in, there's no door," answered Sylfai.

"Come in, come in!" repeated the voice.

Sylfai was just going to say something cross, when she remembered in time.

"Whatever nice thing can I say?" she thought. "Oh, I know. What a pretty yellow colour your house is!" she called.

"Oh, do you like it? I'm so glad," said the voice, sounding very pleased. "As you like the outside, you can see the inside. Climb up the beech tree by the side of the house and get on the roof."

Sylfai climbed up the tree and clambered on to the roof. "Well, dear me," she said, "there *is* only one way of getting into this house it seems—and that is down the chimney!"

She climbed into the chimney, let herself go, and whizz! She found herself sitting inside the house, on a big yellow cushion.

"*That's* the way to come in!" chuckled the dwarf. "I like my house to be different from other people's!"

"Greenskin of the Green Club told me you would show me part of the way to Giant Osta's," said Sylfai.

"Certainly," said the dwarf, a queer, bright-eyed little man. "Follow me."

He lifted up a trap-door, sat down on the edge, and dangled his legs down. "Come after me," he said, and let himself drop.

Sylfai, feeling a little nervous, did the same. She felt herself gliding down a slippery passage—down and down, with little lamps to light the way whizzing past her.

At last she stopped. She found herself by a dark river, which was flowing silently along.

"Here's a boat!" said the dwarf, pulling up a queer-shaped boat to the side. "Get in—you don't need any oars. I'll give you a push off. Goodbye!"

Sylfai jumped in and off sped the boat, rocking from side to side. It floated past great caves, cast dimly lit passages, and at last stopped by a little wooden platform. Sylfai got out and looked around.

"Wherever do I go now!" she thought. "Dear me, what's that?"

She heard a queer rumbling noise coming down the passage in front of her, and then there rolled a bright green ball round a corner, right up to her feet.

"Oh," cried Sylfai, "you're hurting my toes! Do roll off."

The green ball pressed harder. Sylfai was just going to lose her temper when she remembered Corovell's advice again.

"If you don't mind, please will you move yourself?" she said politely. "I'd like to see what you are."

The ball burst open, and out jumped a peculiar creature, with tiny legs, a round body and a round head.

He waved his funny little arms. "I'm the Crawly-wawly Bumpty, he said, "and I always roll on to people's toes, just to see what they say. You're the first person who's ever been polite to me. What can I do for you?"

"What a good thing I was polite!" thought Sylfai. Then she said aloud, "I don't think you're very kind to hurt people's toes, really, you know. Will you tell me where to find Giant Osta?"

"Oh yes. He lives near here. Go up that passage till you come to a door. Knock and Osta will open it." The Crawly-wawly Bumpty jumped into his ball again and rolled merrily off.

"What a funny creature!" said Sylfai, as she went along the passage. After a long while she came to a great blue door, with a tremendous handle. She knocked with her knuckles as loudly as she could.

The door swung open, and a giant peered out and said:

"Who is there?"

"It is only Sylfai, come to try and break Peronel's spell," answered Sylfai, looking in wonder at the huge giant, whose kindly eyes seemed miles above her.

"Oh, splendid!" cried the giant. "I'll pick you up and take you to Peronel." And Sylfai suddenly found herself in the giant's hand, being carefully carried along.

Osta put her down in a great high room. At one end lay a beautiful fairy asleep on a couch. Over her hung a purple card, and Sylfai saw written there:

> "Here Peronel will have to stay,
> Summer, winter, night and day,
> Until the spell is killed away
> By someone who is called Sylfai."

"Oh, what a shame!" cried Sylfai, and she gently bent over sleeping Peronel and kissed her forehead. To her delight Peronel opened her eyes and sat up.

"Oh, I've been under a *horrid* spell," she cried, "and I'm so glad to wake again. How kind you are, Sylfai, to kiss me. Oh, there is Corovell!"

Sylfai turned round, and sure enough there was Corovell, smiling at them both.

"Brave little Sylfai!" she said. "I guessed you would break the spell. Now, let's all go and have a lovely time at the Queen's palace. She wants to see you, Sylfai."

"I'll carry you all there," laughed Giant Osta, picking them all up, and off he went with big strides—and you can just imagine the lovely time Sylfai had with the fairies, and what a lot of adventures she had to tell when she got safely home again!

The Tenth Task

JACK SUDDENLY saw the little yellow door as he wandered across the moors to pick bilberries. It was neatly fitted into the side of the hill he was climbing, and he *almost* didn't see it.

He thought it must be a magic door of some kind, so he felt rather excited. He went right up to it and looked at it. Just an ordinary door it was, but primrose yellow and small. Jack's head would have touched the top. There was no knocker, but a brightly polished handle seemed to invite Jack to turn it and walk in. He did try to turn it and open the door, but nothing happened.

"It must be locked inside," said Jack, disappointed. "What a pity. I can't get in after all."

He tried again, but it was no use, the door was locked. As he looked at it carefully, he suddenly saw a tiny little card pinned by the door, and on it in beautifully printed letters was:

"OPEN ON THURSDAYS AT MIDNIGHT."

"Hooray, I'll come then," cried Jack, "and see what there is to see. Won't I have a lovely time!"

He raced home to his sister Jean, and told her all about his find. "I'm going through that fairy door on Thursday night," he said, "and you'll hear some fine adventures when I come back!"

"Oh, *do* let me come with you," begged Jean. "I want to have adventures too; and, who knows, I might be able to help you somehow, perhaps."

"Pooh," laughed Jack. "You help *me*! I can take care of myself, thank you! I don't want any silly little girls in my adventures. I'm going all by myself."

Jean's curly head drooped sadly as she turned away in disappointment. But when Thursday night came, she packed him up some cakes and went cheerfully to the gate to see him off in the dark, for it was nearly twelve o'clock. "I do hope you'll have some lovely adventures," she said. "And I *do* wish I was coming with you."

"You can next time, perhaps," promised Jack. "You're not clever enough nor old enough to come this first time."

And off he went, whistling loudly.

When he arrived at the little yellow door in the hillside, he found it standing wide open, leading into a narrow passage. This was lighted by a swinging lantern. Jack walked in, feeling just a little bit afraid, but hoping he would have real adventures, with magic in them.

The passage led right into the hill, and suddenly opened out into a large hall, where many kinds of fairy-folk stood about in groups. They were talking and laughing with each other. Jack felt too shy to walk into the hall and speak to the fairies. He hid himself in a little curtained arch at the side of the hall, and watched the fairy-folk in their play.

Soon they began to dance. Jack noticed that they all kept away from one side of the hall, as if they were afraid of something there. He tried to see what it was, but could only catch a glimpse of what looked like a glittering box, standing on a beautifully carved throne. He determined to find out what it was when the fairy-folk had finished dancing. It looked mysterious.

He loved watching the fairies; they were so dainty with their wings outspread and their gossamer frocks, and he was quite sorry when the dancing stopped. One by one the fairies slipped away down the passage and out upon the hillside to their homes, and Jack was left all alone. The hall was dark now, except for one great lamp swinging over the throne on which stood the mysterious box.

Jack crept across to throne, and looked at the box. It was large, and shone in the lamplight like gold. Set around the surface of the lid were rubies and diamonds. The box was locked, but in the lock was a key. Engraven in small letters on the key were these words:

"Beware—Turn Not This Key."

Jack wondered why the key was not to be turned. What would happen if he *did* turn it? He did so badly want to see what was in the box. Perhaps it was a treasure that he could take home and give to Jean.

He suddenly took hold of the key and turned it. He was just lifting the lid up, when—Crash! Bang! Phizz-z-z-z!!

Out of the box sprang a great spirit, with gleaming eyes and coal-black hair. It was much, much taller than Jack, and, with a kick that sent the box flying across the hall, it sat itself down on the big throne and stared at Jack.

"Do you know who I am?" it said with a horrid smile. "I am Zani, the chief of the wicked spirits. I can keep you here as my slave for ever."

Jack threw himself on his knees. "Be merciful to me," he pleaded. "I set you free. Reward me, do not punish me."

Zani laughed. "Very well," he said. "For ten days you may ask me to do ten things for you, one each day. If you find something I cannot do, you may lock me up in the box again. But if you cannot find a task too difficult for me to perform, then I shall take you for my slave for ever."

"All right," said Jack, feeling pleased, and quite sure he could think of things too difficult for anyone to do. "For today's task I want you to give me a pair of wings which I can put on to fly with, and take off if I like."

Zani waved his hand. Immediately there dropped a pair of blue wings down at Jack's feet. He was astonished to find his wish granted so soon, and began to fly about gaily for the first time. He flew home to Jean and told her everything. She was very much surprised and wanted to help Jack to choose some very difficult things. He wouldn't let her, for he said she was not clever enough, and *of course* he could think of something which would prove too difficult for Zani to do.

The next day Jack told the Wicked Spirit to build a great palace for him and Jean, with big gardens full of flowers and fountains. That night a tremendous noise of hammering and clattering was heard, and when day dawned there stood a magnificent palace in its own grounds. Jean and Jack could hardly believe it was theirs. They began to think Zani must be very clever indeed.

The third day Jack asked that the great cellars in the palace should be filled with gold, silver, and precious stones. Zani filled them.

The fourth day, Jack wanted a coat that would make him invisible when he put it on. Zani gave it to him.

The fifth and sixth days Jack told the Wicked Spirit to find the most beautiful ring and the most beautiful necklace in the whole world. These he gave to Jean.

Then Jack began to get worried. For the tenth day was drawing near, and if he could not find something which Zani could not do, he would be his slave for ever.

The seventh day he asked for a lake in his palace grounds, thinking that surely Zani would find this too great a task to do in one day. But no, it was quite easy, or so it seemed, for there stretched a blue lake shimmering in the sunshine.

The eighth and the ninth days Jack asked for a magic sword and for magic shoes of swiftness, knowing that these could only be got from the good fairies, and thinking that Zani would not be allowed to have them. But the Wicked Spirit brought them to him.

On the tenth day, Zani came and said, "What task have you for me today? If you have not one I cannot do, you are my slave, and I shall never let you go.

"I have thought of nothing," said Jack,

trembling. "Let me have until tonight to think."

"No," answered Zani, "you must tell me now! I will wait no longer. You cannot ask me anything I am not able to do."

"Let me say goodbye to my sister, then," cried poor Jack.

"Go, then," said Zani. "You will never see her again." And he laughed horribly.

Jack went into Jean's room and told her that she must say goodbye to him, for he could not think of anything Zani could not do. He must go and be his

slave. Jack trembled as he thought of being in Zani's power.

To his surprise Jean laughed. "Oh," she said, "you thought you were so clever, didn't you? But I can tell you something to ask him which he cannot do."

"What is it? Tell me quickly!" cried Jack.

Jean pulled out a long curly hair from her head.

"Go and tell him to make this straight," she said.

Jack took it and ran back to Zani. "Here is today's task," he cried. "Make this hair of my sister's straight if you can!"

Zani laughed. "What an easy thing to do," he said. "Look, I will make it straight at once."

He pulled the hair straight between his fingers but when he let go, the hair sprang back into its curls. He tried again and again, but each time the hair curled, just as curly hair always will.

He wetted it with water. It curled all the tighter! He ironed it with a great iron. It sprang back into such tight curls that he could hardly pull it straight! He smoothed it, he patted it, he stroked it and shook it, but nothing would make that curly hair go straight. All the day he tried, and when night came he knew he was conquered at last.

With a great mournful howl he fled back to the cave in the hillside, with Jean and Jack after him. They were just in time to see him disappearing into the box. Jean ran forward and turned the key, and there was Zani locked up for years and years to come.

You can guess Jack never said again that he was cleverer than Jean.

Off to the Land of Tiddlywinks

JOHN AND POLLY were climbing up Feraling Hill on a very windy day.

"Goodness! Isn't it windy?" cried John, puffing and panting. "Hullo! What's that lying there?"

Polly looked. "Why, it's a lovely kite!" she said, running up to it. "What a great big one, John. Whoever does it belong to?"

"I don't know. Nobody seems to be here," said John. "Let's fly it, Polly. It ought to go beautifully, in this wind!"

The two children lifted the kite and unbound the string.

Puff! The wind swooped down, caught the kite and swept it high up into the air!

"Isn't it lovely, Polly?" cried John. "Here, hold the kite a minute, whilst I unwind more string!"

Polly held on tightly, but the wind blew and blew, and the kite tugged terribly hard.

"Oh, oh, John, the kite's pulling me off my feet!" cried Polly, running across the grass, dragged by the kite.

"I'll come and help!" shouted John. But alas! Before

he could reach his sister, she was swept off her feet, up into the air, and became a tiny black speck in the distance.

John was dreadfully upset.

"What shall I do? Poor little Polly! What shall I do?" he cried.

"What's the matter?" asked a tiny voice.

John looked round with a jump. He saw a Brownie man sitting on a rock near by.

"Oh, didn't you see what happened to my sister?" he cried. "She's got whisked off by a kite we found lying here."

"That comes of touching what doesn't belong to you!" said the Brownie. "That's a magic kite. It belongs to the Yellow Giant. He *will* be cross when he knows you've used it."

"Oh dear! How dreadful! But what has happened to Polly?" asked John.

"Oh, I expect the kite's taken her to the Land of Tiddlywinks," answered the Brownie. "She'll never come back unless you go and fetch her."

"*Please* tell me the way," begged John, "and I'll go straight off now, and see if I can get her back.'

"Well, go down the Shaking Steps, under that hawthorn bush," advised the Brownie, "until you come to the Rollarounds. I expect they'll help you."

"Thank you!" called John, running to the hawthorn

bush. He looked round it, and at last found a very neat trap-door fitted into the green grass and painted green. He lifted it up, and saw a long flight of yellow steps stretching downwards.

"They're all shaky and jerky!" said John in astonishment, looking at the steps which were continually shaking and very steep.

They made no noise, but John felt very uncomfortable as he went down them. First one shook, then another jerked, and then others wobbled, so that he was really rather afraid of tumbling right down them, and he kept tight hold of the hand-rail.

At last he came to the end, and stepped into a dark passage lit by one dim lamp. It hung just above a door marked:

> ROLLAROUNDS. PLEASE KNOCK.

"Good! Perhaps they'll help me!" thought John, and gave the door a thump. It flew open, and out rolled what looked like big india-rubber balls, bumping against his legs, and making a funny squeaking sound.

"What funny creatures!" thought John.

"Please, could you tell me the way to the Land of Tiddlywinks?" he asked politely.

"Yes, yes!" squeaked the Rollarounds, and they rolled off up the passage at a tremendous rate, John running after them.

At last they came to a large cave, in which sat a solemn dwarf dressed in bright red.

"Good morning!" he said as John approached. "Why have the Rollarounds brought you to me?"

"I asked them the way to the Land of Tiddlywinks," explained John.

"Can you say your A.B.C. backwards?" asked the dwarf.

"I don't know, I never tried," answered John, rather astonished.

"Well, no one can go to Tiddlywinks unless they can say their alphabet backwards," said the dwarf. "It's one of the rules, you know. Let me see if you can."

John tried. He began at Z and went backwards to A very slowly indeed, so as not to make a mistake.

"Hm! It's not very good," said the dwarf. "But I dare say they'll let you in if you say it a bit quicker. You must go by boat to the Crooked Castle, and ask for Giant Certain-Sure. If you're very polite, he'll hand you across to the Land of Tiddlywinks."

"Oh, thank you!" said John. "Where's the boat?"

"Come with me," said the dwarf, going through an

132

archway into another cave. John saw a bright green river flowing through it.

The dwarf whistled.

Down the river came a beautiful boat of purple with no one inside at all.

"Here you are!" said the dwarf. "Get in. It goes by magic. Get out at the Crooked Castle. Goodbye."

"Goodbye!" squeaked all the Rollarounds, nearly rolling into the river.

"Goodbye, and thank you!" shouted John, getting into the boat. Off it floated smoothly, and soon the cave was lost to sight. John was interested in all the other caves they passed. Blue caves, red caves, pink caves, some empty, some full of dancing fairies, some full of sleeping brownies.

At last the boat slipped out into the open air, and floated past fields full of wonderful fairy flowers, which talked to each other and laughed as John floated by.

"Ah! There's Crooked Castle, I'm sure!" suddenly exclaimed John, as he spied a queer, one-sided castle in the distance.

The boat floated on towards it, and at last came to rest beside a little landing-place.

John jumped out. "Thank you, little boat," he said, and ran off to the Crooked Castle. He came to a great open door, and stepped into a cool hall. He looked into all the rooms, but no one was there. At last he came to a big kitchen. There he found a huge giant, sitting by the table with great tears rolling down his face.

"Hullo!" said John. "What are you crying for?"

"Boo-hoo! I can't learn my A.B.C. backwards!" sobbed the giant. "I want to go to the land of Tiddlywinks, where my mother lives, but nobody's allowed to unless they can say their alphabet backwards. I'm certain-sure I knew it five minutes ago, and now I don't."

"Poor Giant Certain-Sure!" said John. "Let me help you. It's a terribly silly rule, but as it *is* a rule, I'll try and help you learn your A.B.C. backwards."

"Thank you. You are very kind," said the giant, cheering up immensely. "Just let me look over it once more, and then I'll say it to you."

He looked at his A.B.C. book and frowned hard. At last he smiled, and looked at John.

"I'm certain-sure I know it now!" he cried. "Z. Y. X. W. … L. B. A. T. …"

"No, no! Quite wrong!" cried John.

"Oh dear! I felt certain-sure I knew it!" cried the giant sadly. "Never mind. I'll try again tomorrow. Can I do anything to help *you* in return for your helping me?"

"Yes, if you don't mind," said John. "I want to go to the Land of Tiddlywinks. The dwarf said you could hand me across."

"I will. Certain-sure I will!" cried the giant. He caught John up in his huge hand, went out into the garden, down a lane, and up to a huge bridge over a great, broad river. He stretched his enormous arm over the river, and put John carefully down on to the other side.

"Goodbye, and thank you, Giant Certain-Sure!" shouted John. He looked around him. He was in the queerest country—the houses were made of tiddlywinks, and the chimneys were tiddlywinks cups!

He was suddenly surrounded by crowds of funny little round-bodied red and white, blue and green creatures—that jumped instead of walked.

"Say your A.B.C. backwards!" cried they.

"Z. Y. X. W.," began John carefully, and got the whole way through without a single mistake.

"Wonderful, wonderful!" cried the Tiddlywinks. "What can we do for you?"

"Where's my sister Polly, who came here with a great kite?" demanded John.

"Here she is! Here she is!" cried the funny little Tiddlywinks as a little girl came running up.

"John! John! I'm so glad to see you!" cried Polly, hugging him. "Do let's go home quickly!"

"Turn round three times, whistle and wish!" said

the Tiddlywinks, dancing round them.

John and Polly turned themselves round three times, whistled and wished, and, hey presto, there they were in their own back garden!

"Oh," cried John, "we'll never meddle with anyone's kite again, will we, Polly?"

"No," said Polly. "But, my goodness, what a lot of adventures we've had. Let's go and tell Mother!" And off they went, and Mother could hardly believe her ears!

The Land of Great Stupids

JOAN AND PAT were quarrelling. Pat had been teaching Joan how to bat at cricket, and Joan would keep holding her bat in the wrong way.

"Joan, you're perfectly silly!" said Pat crossly. "You'll never hit a single ball if you play like that!"

"Well, you're just as silly!" shouted Joan. "Your balls never hit my wicket even though I *do* miss them, so there!"

"Oh, be quiet!" said Pat. "You're just a great stupid, that's what you are, just like all girls. You ought to go to the Land of Great Stupids and live there, that's what *I* think!"

He turned to pick up the ball—and when he turned back again he was astonished to find Joan wasn't there!

"Joan! Joan! Where are you?" he called in surprise.

There was no answer.

"Joan! Joan! Don't be silly. Come back and play!" shouted Pat again.

Still there was no answer. Then suddenly Pat heard a little chuckle in the big chestnut tree above him. He looked up in surprise and saw a queer little gnome's face peeping down at him from between the green leaves.

"Call and call!" said the face. "Call and call! *She* won't hear you! She's gone to the Land of Great Stupids! You said she ought to go there, and she's gone!"

"Oh dear! Oh dear! Poor little Joan!" said Pat. "I didn't mean what I said. I was only just cross. Oh, *do* tell me how to get her back, please!"

"You'll have to go to the Land of Great Stupids yourself, to do that!" answered the gnome, sliding down the tree and standing beside Pat. "You won't enjoy it much, I can tell you!"

"Oh, *that* doesn't matter!" said Pat. "It's my fault Joan went there, and she is my sister, so I *must* look after her. Tell me what to do."

"The Land of Great Stupids belongs to old Witch Wimple," said the gnome. "You'll have to go and ask her if she'll let you go there. I don't expect she will, she's a cross old thing. She may turn you into a spider; you never know."

"Well, I hope she won't," said Pat, feeling rather afraid. "Where does she live?"

"Go to the top of Bracken Hill," said the gnome, "and pick the largest toadstool there. Under it is a trap-door. Go down the steps, and walk on till you come to the Underground Lake. Take a red fairy boat to the Gnome Railway. Then take the train to Yellow Chimney Cottage. That's where Witch Wimple lives."

"Oh, thank you!" said Pat, running off. "It's awfully kind of you to tell me."

He ran down the lane and then up Bracken Hill to the very top.

"Oh, here are the toadstools!" he cried. "I wonder which is the biggest."

He looked all round and at last found one much bigger than the others. He picked it, and looked in

the grass where it had been growing. There he saw a blue ring fixed to the ground.

"I'll pull that ring and I expect I'll lift a trap-door," said Pat excitedly. He caught hold of the blue ring and tugged. Up came a trap-door well hidden in the grass and bracken. Blue steps stretched downwards into darkness.

"Well, here goes!" said Pat, and began climbing down.

They were funny, narrow steps, and he had to hold on to a rail by the side to keep himself from falling. It was very dark, and Pat could not see where he was going.

At last he came to a green lamp and there he met a pixie.

"Good morning," said the pixie. "Where are you going?"

"To the Underground Lake to take a red fairy boat to the Gnome Railway," answered Pat.

"Oh well, take the first turning on the right," said the pixie. "Have you got any money to pay with?"

"No, I haven't," said Pat.

"Well, give me that big toadstool you're carrying, and I'll give you fairy gold," said the pixie. "I can make a spell with your toadstool."

Pat gave it to him and put three pieces of fairy

gold in his pocket. Then he went on again. He took the first turning on the right, and saw a big stretch of gleaming water lying before him.

"How lovely!" cried Pat. "It's a fairy lake, and oh, what darling little boats! They're all shaped like birds!"

So they were. There were swan-boats, duck-boats, robin-boats, and all sorts of other bird-like boats!

"I suppose I take a robin-boat," thought Pat, jingling his fairy gold. "Hi! You robin-boat, come and take me for your passenger."

Up came a red robin-boat, steered by a small blue elf.

"Where to?" he asked.

"The Gnome Railway," answered Pat, jumping in.

"One piece of gold, please," said the elf. Pat gave it to him and the boat started off, floating smoothly and quickly. It went right across the lake passing other boats full of passengers—elves, pixies, gnomes, rabbits, mice and Pat even saw a hedgehog! He was by himself because he was so prickly.

At last they reached a little pier jutting out from the lake-side.

"Here you are!" said the elf. "The train will come right on to the pier. You can get into it there. Goodbye."

Off he went in his little boat again, looking for

another passenger. Pat stood on the pier, waiting. Presently, away in the distance, he saw two little red lights. They drew nearer and nearer, until he saw they belonged to a dear little train, rather like a toy one, coming along quickly and smoothly.

"I suppose it goes by magic as there's no smoke!" thought Pat, as the train ran along the pier and stopped. All kinds of fairy-folk jumped out, and stepped into boats waiting for them. Pat jumped into a carriage and sat down on a cushion on the floor, for there were no proper seats.

The train backed off the pier and then another engine came up and was joined on to the end of the carriages. Off it went into a tunnel, and then through all sorts of lovely caves, and out into the open air. At last it stopped at Dwarf Town Station where lots of dwarfs got in. A little brown dwarf with a long grey beard and twinkling eyes sat on a cushion in Pat's carriage and stared at him.

"What a big hill we're going up!" suddenly said Pat, feeling his cushion sliding down on to the dwarf's.

"Yes, we'll soon be on the top of Blow-away Hill!" said the dwarf. "We'll run down it then at a good pace, I can tell you! You'll lose all your breath!"

Soon the train came to the top of a very, very

windy hill, and began to run down the side of it, between sloping fields of golden buttercups and starry daisies.

Suddenly the dwarf gave a shriek and pointed to something flying through the air.

"Look! Look! There's our driver blown away. I always knew that would happen some day on Blow-away Hill! Now we'll have an accident!" And the dwarf gave another shriek.

Pat clutched the side of the carriage as the train tore down the hill at a terrific speed. Then there came a jolt and a jerk, a tremendous bang, and he found himself rolling head-over-heels on some soft, velvety moss. He got up and felt himself all over.

"Well, I'm not hurt, thank goodness!" he said. "But I wonder what's happened to the dwarf who was with me!"

He ran up to the tumbled-down train. No one seemed a bit hurt, for everyone had fallen on the soft moss that spread all around the railway track. The dwarfs were busy putting the carriages on the lines again.

"What a good thing there's no one hurt!" said Pat, helping two dwarfs to pick up cushions.

"Oh, but that's why the moss is grown round here," said a dwarf. "Didn't you know? The Fairy Queen felt sure there'd be an accident one day, and so she gave orders for moss to be grown at the bottom of Blow-away Hill, just in case!"

Suddenly Pat heard a great noise of crying, and turning round he saw the little dwarf who had been in his carriage.

"Boo-hoo-hoo! Boo-hoo-hoo!" he wept. "I've lost the necklace I was taking to Witch Wimple! It must have fallen out of my pocket in the accident!"

"I'll help you look for it," said Pat kindly, and began searching all around. Just as he was thinking the necklace really must be lost for good and all, he saw it half-buried in a big clump of moss.

"Here it is!" he said, and gave it to the dwarf.

"Oh, thank you," cried the dwarf gladly. "I'm so glad to have it. Where are you going?"

"To old Witch Wimple's," said Pat. "I want to ask her to let me go to the Land of Great Stupids."

"She won't let you do that," said the dwarf. "But look here! I've got an idea. I've got to go there for her, to carry a load of moon beads. I'll ask if you can help me carry it."

So off the two went, over the fields to Yellow Chimney Cottage which stood away in the distance. Old Witch Wimple was standing at the door, shading her eyes with her hands, looking for the dwarf.

"I'm sorry I'm late," called the dwarf as he

hurried up. "The Gnome Train had an accident and I nearly lost your necklace."

"Make haste!" said the witch crossly. "You'll be too late to take those beads to the Land of Great Stupids if you don't hurry!"

Pat and the dwarf ran up to the door and the dwarf gave the witch her necklace. She handed the dwarf a red sack full of something heavy. He tried to lift it and pretended it was too heavy.

"Oh, I say!" he panted. "I think the railway accident must have left me rather weak. Can my friend here help me to carry it?"

"No. I don't allow strangers to go to the Land of Great Stupids," said the witch.

The dwarf tried to lift the sack again, and dropped it.

"Very well," he said. "You'll have to wait till tomorrow, when I get my strength back."

"I *can't* wait till tomorrow, as you very well know," grumbled the witch. "Let your friend help you, then. Get on to the Flying Chair quickly."

The dwarf led Pat to where a big green chair stood in the garden. He sat down on it and made room for Pat. Waving her stick, the witch chanted:

> "*Acrall-da-farray!*
> *Up and away!*
> *To the Land of Great Stupids,*
> *Take them today!*"

Up into the air rose the chair, and Pat held on tightly, afraid he would fall. The chair flew over the hills and fields, across a shining strip of sea, and came slowly down in the middle of a town.

"Here we are!" said the dwarf, getting off the chair. "Now I must hurry. Goodbye and good luck!" And off he ran down the street.

Pat looked round. The town looked very queer. The houses were crooked and old, and the chimneys were all sorts of shapes.

The windows were very tiny and the doorways very big. Queer looking creatures wandered about, with big heads, big ears, big eyes, and big mouths.

"Well, I suppose these are the Great Stupids!" thought Pat. "And they look it too! Why ever don't they shut their mouths! They wouldn't look half so stupid then!"

He went up to one.

"Please could you tell me if there is a little girl called Joan here?" he asked politely.

"I can't speak," said the Great Stupid sadly, and walked off.

"Can't speak!" shouted Pat. "Why, you've just spoken!"

"No, I haven't!" called back the Stupid, with tears in his eyes.

"My goodness! Fancy poor little Joan being here!" said Pat. "I'll go and explore, I think. I wonder who lives in that palace place at the end of the street. It looks a bit better built than any of these awful-looking houses."

He walked up the steps to the palace and into a great hall hung with blue curtains. Then he stood still in the greatest surprise and astonishment. *For there, on a golden throne, sat Joan, his little sister Joan, with a crown on her curly brown hair!*

"Joan! Joan!" shouted Pat, hardly able to believe his eyes. "Is it really you?"

"Pat! Oh, Pat darling! I'm *so* pleased to see you!" cried Joan, suddenly seeing him and running down the hall to meet him. Then she turned to several Great Stupids standing gaping at her in astonishment.

"Leave me for a minute!" she commanded.

"Yes, Your Majesty," they answered, and ran out of the room.

"Oh, Pat! Oh, Pat!" squeaked Joan, with her arms round his neck. "It's lovely to see you! Do take me home."

"What have you got a crown on your head for?" asked Pat.

"Well, when I came here, these Great Stupids asked me all sorts of questions," said Joan. "They asked me why their houses were dark, and I said because they hadn't made their windows big enough. Then they asked me why their houses were so cold, and I told them because they left their big doors open, and of course the wind blew through their houses!"

"What else?" asked Pat.

"They wanted to know why my shoes shone and theirs didn't, and I said because theirs wanted cleaning!" went on Joan. "And, oh, lots of other silly things. Then last of all they asked me if I could say my twelve-times table, and of course I could, and they thought that was WONDERFUL!"

"Did they make you Queen then?" asked Pat.

"Yes. They thought I was so clever. But, oh, Pat darling! I'd rather be called stupid by you than clever by these Great Stupids! Sh! Here they come again. Ask them to let us go home."

In came a crowd of excited Stupids and surrounded Pat.

"Do you come from the Queen's land?" they asked. "Because, if you do, we'll make you King. Come and see if you can answer a difficult question first."

They dragged Pat off and led him to the seashore where lay a crowd of little boats.

"Our boats always sink when we float them in the sea!" they said. "Can you tell us why they do?"

"Why, they're full of holes!" said Pat. "Just look! Of course they get full of water and sink! Have any of you got a cork?"

One of the Stupids gave him one. Pat took out his knife and whittled it at one end. Then he forced the cork into a hole in a boat.

"Now this boat will float!" he said.

"See! It floats beautifully," cried the Stupids joyfully. "We will make you King and you shall stay here always."

"No, thank you," said Pat. "I want to go home with Joan."

"You shan't, you shan't! There's no way of going back!" cried the Stupids, and dragged Pat back to the palace. They put a crown on his head and sat him by Joan.

"Never mind, Joan! We'll escape when it's dark," said Pat. "Look, they're going to give us a feast now! Good! I'm jolly hungry!"

Pat and Joan found it very boring to be King and Queen of the Stupids, for they had to sit and answer questions all day long. They were very glad when night came and they were left alone.

"Quick! Slip out of this window!" whispered Pat.

Both children dropped from the window into a bush, and then ran across the gardens down to the seashore.

"Here's the boat I corked up!" said Pat. "We'll set off in it!"

They jumped in, and Pat began rowing across the water in the moonlight.

Suddenly there came a shout of rage from the shore and crowds of Great Stupids ran down to the sea.

"Come back! Come back," they yelled, "or we'll fetch you back and spank you!"

Then, as they saw Pat was rowing steadily away from them, they jumped into the boats on the beach, and began rowing after Pat's boat. But they had forgotten their boats were full of holes, and before long they filled with water and sank, and the Great Stupids had to wade back to shore, drenched and angry.

"You're too clever for us!" they shouted. "Oh! Why didn't we mend our boats?"

On and on went Pat's boat, until his arms ached. "I do *wish* we were home," he sighed at last.

"Oh! Oh, Pat! What's happening?" suddenly cried Joan. "The boat's flying through the air!"

"It must be a magic boat, making my wish come true!" said Pat. "I expect it's taking us home!"

So it was—for some time later it landed with a little splash in the duckpond in Pat and Joan's own garden!

They got out quickly, very glad to be safe again. Then, with a little click, the boat rose into the air again and disappeared.

"It's gone back to the Land of Great Stupids, I suppose," said Pat. "Well, I hope *we* never go there again, don't you, Joan?"

They went indoors, and Mother was so thankful to see them again.

"I don't like the Land of Great Stupids," she said, when they told her where they had been.

"Oh, look, Mother!" said Pat, feeling in his pockets. "That pixie in Bracken Hill gave me three pieces of gold, and I only used one! I've got two left!"

"We'll hang them on Joan's gold bracelet!" said Mother and they did. And if ever you see a little girl wearing two fairy-gold pieces on her bracelet, ask if her name is Joan, and if she has ever heard of the Land of Great Stupids!

The Prisoners of the Dobbadies

WHEN PETER WAS just finishing his lessons at twelve o'clock, Nurse came running in at the front gate, looking very red.

"Whatever is the matter, Nurse?" asked Mummy.

"Oh dear, oh dear! I've lost Pamela!" said Nurse, sinking down into a chair and looking very miserable.

"Lost Pamela! Where?" exclaimed Mummy.

"We were in the wood together, and Pamela wanted to play at ball. I threw the ball to her and she missed it. She laughed and ran behind a tree to get it, and then," said poor Nurse, "she didn't come back. I looked and called, but it wasn't any good."

They all set off to look for Pamela, but although they called and called, they got no answer, and had to come home without her.

"She must have gone with the fairies," said Peter. "Mummy darling, do let me go and see if I can find her."

Mummy looked at Daddy.

"Shall we let him go and see?" she asked. "He really does see fairies, you know."

"Yes, let him try," said Daddy.

"Oh, thank you, Daddy!" cried Peter, catching up his hat. "I'll go now, and I'm sure I'll bring Pamela back again. Goodbye, Mummy!" and, after a hug, Peter ran out into the garden.

He went straight to the wood, and made his way into the darker parts where the trees grew close together. He came to a little clearing at last, and in the middle grew a ring of white toadstools.

"I'll sit down in the middle of this ring," he said, "for there must be fairies somewhere about here."

He sat down and looked around. Presently he heard a little voice.

"Hullo, Peter!"

"Hullo!" he said. "Where are you? I can't see you."

"Here I am!" laughed the voice, and, looking round, Peter saw a little yellow fairy peeping from behind a tree.

"Come and talk to me," begged Peter. "I want to ask you something."

The fairy came and sat on one of the toadstools. "I'm Morfael," she said. "What is it you want to know?"

"Can you tell me where Pamela is?" asked Peter.

"Yes, Caryll took her off to Fairyland this morning," answered Morfael.

"Whatever for?" asked Peter in surprise.

"Well, you see, the Princess of Dreamland is very ill, and the Wise Elf says she will only get better if she hears the laugh of a little mortal girl. We knew Pamela had the sweetest laugh in the world, so Caryll had orders to take her to Dreamland for a time," explained Morfael.

"Well, I'm going to fetch her back," said Peter, getting up. "Mummy wouldn't mind her making the Princess better, I know, but Pamela is too little to be all alone without anyone she knows. Which is the shortest bay to Fairyland from here?"

"Down Oak Tree House," answered Morfael. "Knock three times. Goodbye! I hope you'll find Pamela," and away she flew.

"Oak Tree House!" said Peter, looking round. "Wherever's that?"

All around him grew beech trees, and he walked about a little, until he came to a big oak tree.

"This must be it," he thought to himself, and knocked three times loudly. A little voice sang a queer little song:

> *"If a fairy's standing there*
> *Enter in, and climb the stair.*
> *If a mortal child you be*
> *Eat an acorn from the tree."*

Peter looked for an acorn, and ate the nut inside the shell.

Immediately everything round him seemed suddenly to grow tremendously big, and made him gasp for breath.

"Goodness me!" said Peter, most astonished. "Why, I've gone small. And oh, how funny! I'm holding on to a grass!"

He looked up at the oak tree. It seemed simply enormous, and its branches looked as if they must touch the sky.

Just in front of him was a little door. It was fitted into the oak tree so beautifully that it was difficult to see it.

Peter pushed at it, and it opened. To his surprise he saw a staircase going up inside the tree.

"What fun!" he said, and carefully shutting the door behind him, he ran up the winding staircase.

At the top he came to a queer little room, rather like an office, in which sat a gnome with a very big head.

"Good morning," said Peter politely, "and thank you for telling me to come in."

"Good morning," said the gnome. "I'm Garin. It isn't often I get a visit from a little boy."

"I'm Peter, and I'm looking for my sister," said Peter. "Could you tell me the way to Fairyland?"

"Yes, certainly. The Yellow Bird will take you straight there," said Garin. "But he doesn't come till two o'clock. I'm just going to have my dinner. Will you have some with me?"

"I'd *love* to," answered Peter. "I haven't had any, and I'm terribly hungry."

"Sit down then," said Garin. He bustled about, and soon had the queerest-looking dinner ready. Peter enjoyed it thoroughly and told him all about Pamela, and how he was going to look for her.

"Well, I don't think you'll find it quite so easy as you think," said Garin, looking grave. "The

Dobbadies don't like the Princess of Dreamland, because she won't let them live in her country, they're too mischievous. And if *they* hear that Pamela is going to cure the Princess, they may take it into their heads to capture Pamela before she gets to Dreamland."

"Oh dear! Do you really think so?" asked Peter, putting down his glass of honey-dew drink in dismay.

"Well, I don't know," answered Garin, "but the Yellow Bird will tell us all the news when he comes. Anyway, I'll give you a piece of advice, which will always be of help to you in Fairyland."

"Oh, thank you!" said Peter gratefully. "I'll be sure to remember it."

"Well, it's this," said Garin. "Whenever you feel impatient, or cross, don't think about it, and instead, look round you and see if you can find something beautiful. If you do that you'll be all right—but if you don't, things will go wrong and you won't find Pamela."

"Well, that sounds easy enough," said Peter.

"Hark! What was that?"

A noise of footsteps was heard on the stairs.

"Oh, that's only the people who want to go to Fairyland at two o'clock," explained Garin, clearing away the dinner.

Then into the little room came all sorts of fairies and gnomes, talking and laughing with each other.

Suddenly a little bell tinkled.

"There's the Yellow Bird," exclaimed Garin. "Come along, everybody."

He opened a door, and Peter saw leaves waving in the wind.

"Why, it's the outside of the tree," he exclaimed.

Everyone walked along a broad branch until they came to where a large and beautiful yellow bird was waiting.

"Good afternoon," said the Yellow Bird. "Is everybody here?"

"Yes," said Garin. "Get on, Peter. Any news, Yellow Bird?"

"Yes," answered the bird. "The Dobbadies have captured the Princess of Dreamland, and a little girl called Pamela, who was with her, and nobody knows where they've gone."

"Oh dear! Oh dear!" said Peter. "That's just what you said might happen, Garin. *Now* what am I to do?"

"Are you Pamela's brother?" asked the Yellow Bird. "Well, get on my back, and I'll try and think of a plan for you as we go along."

Peter got on, and all the fairies and gnomes climbed up too. It was a very good thing the Yellow Bird had such a broad back, Peter thought.

Just as they were going to start, someone came running across the branch.

"Stop, stop!" she cried. "I'm coming too."

"Hurry up, hurry up, Little Miss Muffet," called Garin. "You're very late."

"I'm *so* sorry," panted Miss Muffet, a little girl about the same size as Peter, "but that horrid spider came and frightened me again and I dropped my bowl and spoon, and had to go back and find them."

She sat down beside Peter. The Yellow Bird spread his wings and off he flew into the air.

"Goodbye, goodbye!" called Garin.

Peter clung on to the bird's feathers, and thought flying was simply glorious. He was sorry when the Yellow Bird kept stopping at various places, to let the fairies, the gnomes, or the rabbit get down.

At last only he and Miss Muffet were left.

"Have you thought of a plan yet?" asked Peter.

"Yes. I think you had better go to the Hideaway House, and ask the Wise Elf there to help you. He will know what to do," answered the bird.

"I'll go with you," said Miss Muffet. "I've got to get off near there."

At last the Yellow Bird slowed down and came to a stop.

"Here you are," he said. "The Hideaway House is in that wood over there."

"Oh, thank you," said Peter, getting off. He helped Miss Muffet off, and they both went into the wood.

Suddenly Miss Muffet gave a scream.

"Oh! Oh! There's that horrid spider again!"

Peter saw an immense brown spider coming towards Miss Muffet.

"Quick, run!" he shouted, catching hold of her hand and dragging her behind a tree.

Then he bravely caught up a dead tree-branch, and turned to face the spider.

"I'm going to *kill* you if you frighten Miss Muffet any more," he said, and lifting up his stick, he brought it down on the spider's hairy back with a tremendous whack.

To his great astonishment, the spider sat down and began to cry.

"Oh, oh, oh!" he sobbed. "You are unkind to me. I'm not really a spider, I'm a fairy changed into one. And I love Miss Muffet, but directly I sit down beside her, I'm so ugly, I frighten her away. And now you've hurt me dreadfully."

"I'm awfully sorry," said Peter, "but how *was* I to know that you weren't a spider? Wait a minute, and I'll tell Miss Muffet."

He ran to where she was hiding.

"It isn't a spider, it's a poor fairy changed into

one," he told her, "and he loves you and doesn't want to frighten you."

"Is it *really*?" asked Miss Muffet. "Then I don't mind so much. I'll go and stroke the poor thing."

She ran to where the spider was still crying large tears on to the grass, and stroked him. He stopped crying at once, and cried out:

"A thousand thanks to you, little boy. You have done me a great kindness in making Miss Muffet friends with me. Any time you want help, clap your hands three times, and call for Arran the Spider."

"Thank you, I will," said Peter, "but now, goodbye, I'm going to the Wise Elf in Hideaway House."

"We'll stay and help you catch it, then," said Miss Muffet, who seemed to have lost all fear of the spider.

"*Catch* it! Whatever *do* you mean?" exclaimed Peter, astonished.

Miss Muffet laughed. "Ah! You'll see," she said.

"There's Hideaway House," said Peter, running towards a queer little wooden house. But just as he got near to it, it disappeared!

"Oh!" cried Peter, amazed and stopping still. "It's gone!"

"It's behind you, Peter," laughed Miss Muffet. Sure enough it was.

"However did it get there?" said Peter, going towards it again. But just as he reached the front door, it vanished again.

"I don't like this sort of house," said Peter, looking puzzled. "Where's it gone to now?"

"Over in that corner," said the spider, pointing to it with one of his eight legs.

"I'll try again," said Peter, and ran over to the little house, but no—directly he reached it, it disappeared once more.

"This is stupid," stormed Peter, feeling quite cross.

"We'll help you," said Miss Muffet. "Directly it comes near us, we'll catch hold of it."

But try as they would, the Hideaway House always got away, and when they looked round, there it was, standing behind them somewhere.

"It's got a very good name," said Peter, "but it's the stupidest house I *ever* saw."

He stared at the house and frowned hard. He felt very impatient and cross. Then he suddenly remembered Garin's advice.

"He said I was to look round for something beautiful whenever I felt cross," said Peter to himself. "Very well, I will."

He looked all round the wood, and his eye caught sight of something blue.

"What's that?" he said, and ran to see. "Oh, 'tis a perfectly lovely little flower!" he called to Miss Muffet. "Come and look, it's the prettiest I ever saw."

Miss Muffet looked at it.

"It's the rarest flower in Fairyland," she said. "What a good thing you saw it! Now, all you've got to do is to pick it, and stand in the middle of the clearing here and shout out to the Wise Elf that you've found the blue Mist-flower! He's always wanting it for his magic spells."

Peter picked it, and stood upright.

"Wise Elf in Hideaway House!" he called. "I've found the blue Mist-flower! Do you want it?"

At once the door of Hideaway House opened, and an Elf with large wings, large eyes and large ears stood on the doorstep.

"Come in! Come in," he called, "and bring the Mist-flower with you."

"Goodbye," cried Miss Muffet and the spider. "We're so glad you've got the Hideaway House at last!" and off they went into the wood.

Peter ran across to the Hideaway House, and to his delight it stood still this time and didn't disappear. He went inside the front door and found himself in a dark room at one end of which sat the Wise Elf.

"Good afternoon," he said. "I am glad to see you."

"Good afternoon," said Peter. "This is a funny sort of house to live in. If I hadn't remembered Garin's advice to stop being cross and look round for something beautiful, I would never have got here."

"Possibly not," said the Wise Elf, nodding at Peter. "Being impatient and cross never did *anybody* any good. Give me that Mist-flower, please."

Peter handed it to him.

"Please could you tell me how I can find the Dobbadies?" he asked.

"Well," said the Wise Elf, putting on a large pair of spectacles, and taking down a book. "Well, I can tell you which way to go, and as you've been clever enough to find exactly the flower I've been wanting for six months, I shall be glad to show you part of the way. Let me see. Let me see!" and he turned over the pages of his book.

"Ah, here we are," he said at last, coming to a page on which was a queer map. "Yes, I thought so—the Dobbadies live on the north side of Dreamland—now, how can you get there? Ummm-m, um-m-m, let me see. Yes, I think I can tell you."

"Oh, thank you," said Peter gratefully.

"You had better go through the Underground Caves to the Sleepy Sloos, then you must get them to take you to the Rushing Lift to Cloudland. From

Cloudland you can get straight down to Giant Roffti's, and he will carry you across to where the Dobbadies live. Then you must find out how to rescue Pamela."

"It sounds rather hard," said Peter, feeling a little dismayed.

"If you make up your mind to do it, you *will* do it," said the Wise Elf, looking over the tops of his spectacles at Peter.

"Then I'm *going* to do it," said Peter, jumping up. "Would you mind showing me part of the way, Wise Elf?"

"Certainly," answered the Elf. "I can take you as far as the entrance to the Underground Caves."

"Thank you," said Peter. "I'm really awfully obliged to you."

The Wise Elf bent down and pulled a mat up from the floor. A trap-door lay underneath.

"Help me pull it up," said the Elf. He and Peter tugged it upright, and Peter saw a long flight of steps stretching downwards.

The Wise Elf ran down the steps, and Peter followed. After they had gone down about a hundred, they came out into a large passage, which was lighted with green lamps.

"Oh, I do believe it's an underground railway. How lovely!" cried Peter.

"Quite right," said the Elf. "Ah, look! The lamps have changed to red. That means the train is coming."

Then suddenly, gliding out of the darkness, came such a small engine that Peter thought it must be a toy one.

"It's run by magic," explained the Wise Elf. "It's stopping for us, so we must get in quickly."

He helped Peter into a funny-looking carriage. There were no seats, but just fat cushions on the floor.

"Good afternoon," said the Wise Elf politely to the folk inside. He chose a fat green cushion to sit on, and pointed out a mauve one.

The carriage was full of fairy-folk of all kinds. Goblins, gnomes, fairies, and pixies were there, all chattering gaily to each other.

"Where are you going to?" they asked Peter.

"To the Underground Caves," he answered. "Where are *you* all going to?"

"We're all going to the Gnome King's party," answered a very beautifully-dressed fairy.

The train ran along quietly, past big bowl-shaped lamps lighting up the passage, and at last came to a stop at a little platform.

"Here we are!" said the Wise Elf. He and Peter got out, and the train went on into the darkness.

"Goodbye, goodbye," called all the folk who were

going to the party.

The Wise Elf went to a door on the platform and opened it. It led into a dark cave, lit only by one lantern in the middle.

"Here I must leave you," said the Elf. "If you wait here for a little while, you will see the entrance to the Underground Caves. I hope you will find Pamela. Goodbye."

"Goodbye!" called Peter, feeling rather lonely as he saw the Elf run back to the platform to catch the next train back.

He waited in the dark cave for about ten minutes and then suddenly saw a shiny silver rope coming slowly down from the ceiling.

"This must be something to do with the cave's entrance," said Peter, and as the rope reached him, he caught hold of it and gave it a pull.

Immediately one side of the cave split open and formed a great archway, leading into another cave!

"Hurray!" cried Peter, running through. "Here's the entrance at last!"

He looked all round him, and found he was in a tremendously large cave, lighted with pink lights. No one was there. There was an archway leading into another cave. Peter ran into it. It was lighted with mauve lights, and was smaller than the first.

"Why, *this* one's got an archway leading into

another cave," cried Peter, "and they're all empty."

He ran into the next one and looked all round. It had orange lights and was still smaller.

On and on Peter went, into smaller and smaller caves, each lighted differently. At last he came to the smallest cave of all, which had big blue lamps swinging from the ceiling.

"Oh, there really *is* somebody here!" said Peter, feeling very pleased.

All around the cave were lying mouse-like creatures with large ears, and all were fast asleep.

"Hullo! Are you the Sleepy Sloos?" asked Peter loudly.

No one stirred.

"I say! I want to go to Cloudland," called Peter, "so will you help me, please?"

Still no one stirred, but Peter somehow felt quite certain some of the Sleepy Sloos were awake, but were too lazy to help him.

"Wake up! Wake up!" shouted Peter, shaking the one nearest him.

But it was all no good. Peter felt very cross and most impatient, and was just going to stamp round the cave in a temper, when he suddenly remembered Garin's advice again.

"Oh dear, there *isn't* anything beautiful to look at here!" he grumbled. But he determined to have a good look round the cave all the same.

"Hullo! What's that?" he said, tugging at something that twinkled in a crack of the cave rock. "What a beautiful stone! It's a diamond, I do believe."

"What?"

"What's that?"

"What have you got?"

All the Sleepy Sloos had suddenly waked up and were shouting at Peter.

"Hurray! He's found the magic stone we lost last week! How lovely!" cried they, and crowded round Peter.

"Oh," said Peter, "so you've waked up at last! What a good thing I took Garin's advice! If I give you back your stone, will you stay awake long enough to show me the Rushing Lift to Cloudland?"

"Yes, yes, yes!" cried the Sleepy Sloos.

Peter gave them the stone, which glittered and twinkled just as though it were alive.

The Sleepy Sloos took paws and danced in a ring and sang:

> "Rushing Lift
> You must come down
> And take this boy
> To Cloudland Town."

Then crash! The roof of the cave split open and down there came a bright orange chair, swinging on purple ropes.

"Get in, get in," cried the Sleepy Sloos. "We want to go to sleep. Goodbye!" and they all settled down again and began to snore.

Peter got into the orange chair, and whizz-z-z! He shot right up into the air at a most tremendous pace! When it stopped, he got out and found himself on a great soft cloud.

"Goodness me! *Now* where do I go?" he said.

"Where would you like to go?" asked a voice.

"Who are you speaking?" asked Peter, looking all round.

"I'm the cloud. I'll take you wherever you like," answered the voice.

"Then take me down to Giant Roffti's, please," said Peter, feeling most astonished to hear a cloud speak.

"Very well. Sit down and hold tight," commanded the cloud. Peter did so, and felt the cloud slowly sink down, down, down, through the air. It seemed simply ages before it stopped.

"Here we are!" at last said the cloud. "We're in Roffti's backyard. He'll be in the kitchen, I expect. Goodbye!" And as Peter scrambled off the cloud, it swiftly rose again up into the sky.

Peter was in a huge backyard, full of the largest dustbins he had ever seen. Near by was a great open door.

"I suppose that's the kitchen," thought Peter, and walked boldly in.

Inside he found a huge giant busy putting tremendous cakes into an oven. The giant looked very hot and very tired, Peter thought.

"Please," said Peter, "could you take me to the Dobbadies?"

"Bless me! Bless me!! Bless me!!!" exclaimed the giant, dropping a tray of cakes in amazement. "How you made me jump!"

"I *am* so sorry," said Peter, feeling very uncomfortable as he saw the cakes rolling all over the floor.

"Oh, never mind," puffed the giant, looking hotter than ever. "Accidents *will* happen!"

"Are you very busy?" asked Peter politely.

"Yes. There's a grand party on in Giantland today and I'm baking some extra cakes," answered the giant, picking up the dropped cakes.

"What a lot of parties are on today!" said Peter.

"Yes, the Dobbadies are going to this one," said the giant. "So it's no good my taking you to see them today."

"Oh, good!" cried Peter. "You see, I want to

rescue my sister and the Princess of Dreamland from the Dobbadies, and it would be much easier if they're not there!"

"Right! Come along, quickly!" cried Roffti, catching Peter up in one hand. He rushed out into the garden, jumped across a large pond, ran down a dark lane, and into a broad drive. At the

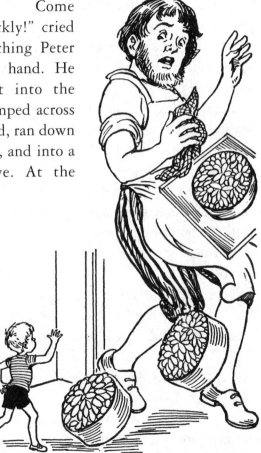

end stood a great sparkling palace, with thousands of windows.

"That's where the Dobbadies live!" said Roffti. "Now, what's your sister's name?"

"Pamela," said Peter, still dangling in the giant's huge hand.

"Pamela! Pamela! Pamela!" roared the giant.

At a tiny window near the roof a little girl's curly head peeped out.

"There she is!" shouted Peter excitedly. Roffti lifted Peter up and put him on the window-sill. To Peter's great delight there was Pamela, lifting her arms to him in joy.

"Peter! Oh, I *am* glad you've come!" she cried. "And here's the Princess, she's a prisoner too."

Peter clambered into the room, and saw a beautiful lady sitting on a chair, and looking very miserable.

"Cheer up!" he cried excitedly. "I've come to rescue you while the Dobbadies are at the party!"

"Come on, then," said Pamela, running to the door.

All three raced down the stairs and out into the garden.

"Hush!" suddenly cried the Princess as a queer cloppity noise reached them.

"Oh, oh, it's the Dobbadies!" whispered Pamela.

Sure enough it was! There they were, little gnome-like creatures, but with three legs instead of two, pouring into the garden, back from the party early.

"Oh dear! What *can* I do?" thought poor Peter, looking desperately around. "I can't fight them *all*!"

Suddenly he remembered Arran the Spider.

"*He'll* help me, of course!" he cried, and clapping his hands three times loudly, he cried, "Arran, Arran the Spider! Come and help me, Arran!"

All the Dobbadies crowded round shouting: "They're escaping! Catch them!"

Then, just as they caught hold of Pamela and the Princess, Peter gave a shout:

"Hurrah! Here's good old Arran! And he's brought Miss Muffet, too!"

Arran, the huge spider, ran rapidly into the garden, carrying Miss Muffet on his back.

The Dobbadies let go Pamela and the Princess with cries of alarm. "What is it? What is it?" they cried.

"Something that will *eat* you!" cried Arran, as he jumped at them.

"Oh, oh, oh!" cried the Dobbadies, and fled into the palace for all they were worth.

"Quick!" cried Arran. "Run whilst you've a chance. Miss Muffet will show you the way, and I'll come last and eat up the Dobbadies that follow!"

Little Miss Muffet ran down a passage into a large cave, and the others followed her. A river ran through the cave, and there was a little boat moored to a yellow post.

"Jump in, jump in!" cried Arran. "The Dobbadies are coming again."

All of them jumped in the little rocking boat, and just as a crowd of three-legged Dobbadies came rushing into the cave, Arran pushed off.

"Now we're safe," he said, as the boat raced off on the underground river. "There's no other boat for the Dobbadies to take."

So the Dobbadies were left behind, shouting and screaming because the prisoners had escaped.

"Oh, thank you for coming to our help, Arran," said Peter, stroking the huge spider.

"Very pleased to," said Arran. "You made little Miss Muffet friends with me, and I could never forget that."

"Where do you want to go to?" asked Miss Muffet.

"Oh, *home*, please," said Pamela, "because I've made the Princess well now, and I want my mummy."

The boat went on and on until at last the river flowed out into open fields.

"Why, we've come to a pond!" exclaimed Peter, as the boat came to a stop.

"And it's *our* pond, in *our* garden!" cried Pamela. "But I *know* there isn't a river into it!"

"Ah, it's magic, you see," said Arran. "It'll be gone tomorrow. Now, goodbye; you'll see us again sometime. I'm going to take the Princess back to Dreamland."

"Goodbye, goodbye!" shouted Pamela and Peter, running up the garden path.

"Mummy, Mummy!" cried Pamela, as Mummy and Daddy came running to meet them.

"Oh, Peter, you *are* clever and brave!" said Mummy, when all the story had been told, and everyone had been hugged and kissed a hundred times over.

"Come and look at the magic river, Daddy," begged Peter, running into the garden.

But alas! It was gone.

"Never mind," said Peter, "we've had some *glorious* adventures, and when the river comes again one day, we'll have some more!"